Praise for August Heat

'Andrea Camilleri is one of Italy's
he's on top form in his latest Inspecto.
Sunday Times

'This is Inspector Montalbano's tenth outing and cements
Camilleri's reputation as the finest living Italian crime writer'
Daily Mirror

'The seal of the best foreign crime writing is as much the
stylish prose as the unfamiliar settings. When both ingredients
are presented with the expertise shown by Andrea Camilleri,
the result is immensely satisfying'
Independent

'The climax of *August Heat* is brilliant but for the
inspector, sad, and, unusually, engaging of his emotions.
This does not mean that Camilleri has lost any of the wit, fun
and exuberance of his previous novels. Montalbano's added
maturity has merely enhanced the excellence of the series'
Marcel Berlins, *The Times*

'The popularity of Camilleri's clever, bitter-sweet novels
comes from their human comedy, their commitment-phobic
central figure, and from the quality of the writing'
Times Literary Supplement

'This welcome addition to an excellent series is a brilliant,
blackly comic read with an all-too-human protagonist
. . . a cut above the average thriller'
Waterstone's Books Quarterly

AUGUST HEAT

Andrea Camilleri is one of Italy's most famous contemporary writers. His Montalbano series has been adapted for Italian television and translated into several languages. He lives in Rome.

Stephen Sartarelli is an award-winning translator. He is also the author of three books of poetry, most recently *The Open Vault*. He lives in France.

ANDREA CAMILLERI

AUGUST HEAT

Translated by Stephen Sartarelli

PICADOR

First published 2009 by Penguin Books, a member of Penguin Group (USA) Inc., New York

First published in Great Britain 2009 by Picador

This edition published 2013 by Picador
an imprint of Pan Macmillan, a division of Macmillan Publishers Limited
Pan Macmillan, 20 New Wharf Road, London N1 9RR
Basingstoke and Oxford
Associated companies throughout the world
www.panmacmillan.com

ISBN 978-1-4472-4148-5

1 3 5 7 9 8 6 4 2

A CIP catalogue record for this book is available from
the British Library.

Typeset by SetSystems Ltd, Saffron Walden, Essex
Printed in the UK by CPI Group (UK) Ltd, Croydon, CR0 4YY

ONE

He was sleeping so soundly that not even cannon-fire could have woken him. Well, maybe not cannon-fire, but the ring of the telephone, yes.

Nowadays, if a man living in a civilized country (ha!) hears cannon-blasts in his sleep, he will, of course, mistake them for thunderclaps, gun salutes on the feast day of the local saint, or furniture being moved by the upstairs neighbours, and go on sleeping soundly. But the ring of the telephone, the triumphal march of the mobile, or the doorbell, no: those are sounds of summons to which the civilized man (ha-ha!) has no choice but to surface from the depths of slumber and answer.

So, Montalbano got out of bed, glanced at the clock, then at the window, from which he gathered that it was going to be a very hot day, and went into the dining room where the telephone was ringing wildly.

'Salvo! Where were you? I've been trying to get hold of you for half an hour!'

1

'I'm sorry, Livia. I was in the shower so I couldn't hear the phone.'

First lie of the day.

Why did he tell it? Because he was ashamed to tell her he had still been asleep? Or because he didn't want to embarrass her by telling her she'd woken him? Who knows?

'Did you go to look at the house?'

'Livia! It's barely eight o'clock!'

'I'm sorry. I'm just so desperate to know if it's all right . . .'

The whole business had started about two weeks before when he'd had to tell Livia that, contrary to plan, he would not be able to leave Vigàta for the first half of August because Mimì Augello had been forced to take his holiday earlier than expected due to complications with his in-laws. But the change had not produced the calamitous results he had feared. Livia was very fond of Beba, Mimì's wife, and of Mimì himself. She had complained a little, of course, but Montalbano had thought that would be the end of it. He had been wrong. Way off the mark, in fact. The following evening Livia had called back with a surprise request.

'I'm looking for a house, straight away, two bedrooms, living room, by the sea, in your area.'

'I don't understand. Why can't we just stay at my place in Marinella?'

'You can be so stupid, Salvo, when you put your mind

to it! I meant a house for Laura, her husband and their little boy.'

Laura was Livia's dearest friend, the one to whom she confided her Joyful and not-so-Joyful Mysteries.

'They're coming here?'

'Yes. Do you mind?'

'Not at all. I think Laura and her husband are very nice, you know that. It's just that . . .'

'It's just what?'

Jesus, what a pain!

'I was hoping we could finally spend a little more time together, just the two of us, alone—'

'Ha-ha-ha-ha!'

A laugh rather like that of the witch in *Snow White and the Seven Dwarfs*.

'What's so funny?'

'What's so funny is that you know damn well the only one who's going to be alone is me – me and nobody else – while you're spending your days and maybe even your nights at the station working on the latest murder.'

'Come on, Livia, it's August. With this kind of heat, even the killers down here wait until autumn.'

'Was that a joke? Am I supposed to laugh?'

Thus had begun the long search for a house, with the help – inconclusive – of Catarella. 'Chief, I tink I gotta place like you's lookin' for, out by Pezzodipane.'

'But Pezzodipane's six miles from the sea!'

'Iss true, but to make up for it, there's a artifishy lake.'

Or: 'Livia, I found a lovely little apartment in a sort of block near—'

'A *little* apartment? I told you clearly I want a house.'

'Well, an apartment's a house, isn't it? What else is it? A tent?'

'No, an apartment is not a house. It's you Sicilians who confuse the matter by calling an apartment a house, whereas when I say "house", I mean "house". Would you like me to be more specific? I want you to find a free-standing, single-family residence.'

The estate agents in Vigàta laughed in his face.

'What — you think you can come in on the sixteenth of July and have found a house by the sea for the first of August? It was all let a long time ago.' But they'd told him to leave his telephone number. If, by chance, somebody cancelled at the last minute, they would let him know. And a miracle happened, at the very moment he had given up hope.

'Hello — Inspector Montalbano? This is the Aurora estate agency. A nice little villa by the sea has come free, the sort of thing you were looking for. It's at Marina di Montereale, in the Pizzo district. But you'd better come over quickly, because we're about to close.'

He'd left in the middle of an interrogation and rushed to the agency. From the photos it was exactly what Livia wanted. He'd arranged that Mr Callara, the agency boss, would pick him up the following morning at around nine o'clock to show him the house, which was less than six miles from Marinella.

Montalbano realized that six miles on the road to Montereale at the height of summer could as easily mean five minutes as two hours, depending on traffic. Too bad. Livia and Laura would have to make do. It couldn't be helped.

The following morning, as soon as he got into the car, Callara started to talk and didn't stop. He began with recent history, recounting how the house had been let to a certain Jacolino, a clerk in Cremona who had paid the required deposit. But just last night, Jacolino had phoned the agency saying his wife's mother had had an accident so they couldn't leave Cremona for the time being. And the agency had rung him, Montalbano, straight away.

Next, Mr Callara had delved into history. That was, he had told him in full detail how and why the house had been built. Some six years ago, an old fellow of about seventy, who went by the name of Angelo Speciale – Monterealese by birth, but an emigrant to Germany, where he'd worked for the rest of his life – had decided to build himself this house so he could come back to his home town once and for all with his German wife. This German wife, whose name was Gudrun, was a widow with a twenty-year-old son called Ralf. Got that? Got it. Well, Angelo Speciale had come to Montereale in the company of his stepson, Ralf, and gone around for a month, looking for the right location. When he'd found it, and bought it, he went to see Mr Spitaleri, the developer, and asked him to draw up the plans. He had waited a year and more for the construction to be completed. Ralf had stayed with him all the time.

Then they went back to Germany to have their furniture and other possessions shipped to Montereale. But a weird thing happened. Since Angelo Speciale didn't like flying, they had taken the train. When they got to Cologne station, however, Mr Speciale couldn't find his stepson, who had been travelling in the bunk above his. Ralf's suitcase was still in the compartment, but there was no trace of him. The night conductor said he hadn't seen anyone leave the train at any of the earlier stops. In short, Ralf had disappeared.

'Did they ever find him?'

'Would you believe it, Inspector? They never did! From that moment on, no one ever heard from him again.'

'And did Mr Speciale move into the house?'

'That's the best part! He never did! Poor Mr Speciale, he hadn't been back in Cologne a month before he fell down the stairs, hit his head and died!'

'What about the twice-widowed Mrs Gudrun? Did she come down here to live?'

'What was she going to do here, poor thing, without her husband or son? She called us three years ago and told us to let the house. And since then we have, but only in the summer.'

'Why not during the rest of the year?'

'It's too isolated, Inspector. You'll see for yourself.'

It was indeed isolated. One got there by turning off the provincial road on to an uphill track, with only a rustic cottage, another slightly less rustic cottage and, at the end, the house. There were hardly any trees or other vegetation. The entire area was parched by the sun. But the moment one arrived at the house, which was at the top of a hill, the view changed. It was breathtaking. Below, extending in both directions, there was a beach of golden sand, dotted here and there with a few umbrellas; and in front, the clear, open, welcoming sea. The house, which was all on one floor, had two bedrooms, a big one with a double bed and a smaller one with a single, a spacious living room with rectangular windows looking on to nothing but sea and sky, certainly not a television. The kitchen was sizeable and equipped with an enormous fridge. There were even two bathrooms. And a terrace that was perfect for open-air dining in the evening.

'I like it,' said the inspector. 'How much is it?'

'Well, Inspector, normally we don't let a house like this for only two weeks, but since it's for you ...'

He spat out a figure that was like a cudgel to the head. But Montalbano didn't feel a thing. After all, Laura was rich and could play her part in alleviating the poverty of southern Italy. 'I like it,' he repeated.

'Naturally, there will be some additional expenses—'

'Naturally, there *won't* be any additional expenses,' said Montalbano, who didn't want to be taken for a fool.

'Okay, okay.'

'How do you get down to the beach?'

'Well, you go through the little gate on the terrace, then walk about ten yards to a small stone staircase that leads down to it. There are fifty steps.'

'Could you give me about half an hour?'

Callara looked befuddled. 'If you keep it to half an hour . . .' he said.

From the moment he'd seen it, Montalbano had wanted to dive into that sea, which seemed to be beckoning him, and go for a long swim. He swam in his underpants.

When he returned, the sun had dried him off by the time he had climbed the fifty steps.

✶

On the morning of 1 August, Montalbano went to Palermo's Punta Raisi airport to meet Livia, Laura and her son, Bruno, a little boy of three. Guido, Laura's husband, would come later by train, bringing a car and their baggage across the strait. Bruno was one of those children incapable of sitting still for two consecutive minutes. Laura and Guido were a little concerned that the boy still didn't talk and communicated only with gestures. He didn't even like to draw or scribble like other children of his age; to make up for it, however, he was a master at breaking the *cojones* of all creation.

They went to Marinella, where Adelina had prepared

lunch for the whole gang. But Montalbano's housekeeper had already gone when they arrived, and Montalbano knew he wouldn't see her again for the remainder of Livia's fifteen days there. Adelina had a deep antipathy towards Livia, and the feeling was mutual.

Guido stumbled in around one o'clock. They ate, and immediately afterwards, Montalbano got into his car with Livia to lead the way for Guido, in his car with his family. When Laura saw the house, she was so excited she hugged and kissed Montalbano. Bruno indicated that he wanted the inspector to hug him too. But as soon as Montalbano picked him up, the child spat the sweet he was sucking into the inspector's eye.

They agreed that the following morning Livia would come to see Laura in Salvo's car, since he could get a lift to work in a patrol car, and would stay for the day. That evening, when he finished work, Montalbano would get somebody to drive him to Pizzo, and together they would decide where to go out to eat.

That seemed to the inspector an excellent plan, since it would allow him at lunchtime to feast on whatever he liked best at Enzo's trattoria.

*

The troubles at the beachside house in Pizzo began on the morning of the third day. When Livia went to see her friend, she found the place upside-down: clothes had been pulled out of the armoire and piled on the terrace chairs, mattresses pushed up under the windows of the bed-rooms, kitchen utensils strewn across the ground in the parking area in front of the entrance. Bruno, naked, with the garden hose in hand, was doing his best to soak the clothes, mattresses and sheets. The moment he saw her he tried to soak Livia too, but she, knowing him well, stepped out of the way. Laura was lying on a deck-chair next to the low terrace wall, a wet rag over her forehead.

'What on earth is going on?'

'Have you been inside the house?'

'No.'

'Look inside from the terrace, but be careful not to go in.'

Livia went in through the little terrace gate, and looked into the living room.

The first thing she noticed was that the floor had turned almost black.

The second thing she noticed was that the floor was alive – it was moving in all directions. After which she didn't notice anything, having understood what she had seen. She screamed and ran off the terrace.

'Cockroaches! Thousands of them!'

'This morning, at the crack of dawn,' said Laura, with great effort, as if lacking even the breath to go on living, 'I got up to get a drink of water, and I saw them, but there weren't so many of them then … so I woke up Guido, and we tried to salvage whatever we could, but we soon gave up. They kept coming up out of a crack in the living-room floor ...'

'And where's Guido now?'

'He went to Montereale. He rang the mayor, who was very nice. He should be back at any moment.'

'Why didn't he try Salvo?'

'He said he couldn't bring himself to call the police over an invasion of cockroaches.'

Some fifteen minutes later Guido pulled up, followed by a car from the mayor's office carrying four pest-controllers, armed with cans of poison and brooms.

Livia took Laura and Bruno back to Marinella, while Guido stayed behind to coordinate the disinfestation and clean the house. Around four o'clock in the afternoon he, too, appeared at Marinella.

'They were coming out of that crack in the floor. We sprayed two whole cans down there, then cemented it up.'

'There wouldn't happen to be any more of those cracks, would there?' Laura asked, seeming unconvinced.

'Don't worry, we looked everywhere,' said Guido, settling the matter. 'It won't happen again. We can go home without any anxiety.'

'Why did they all come out like that?' Livia cut in.

'One of the pest-controllers explained that the house must have shifted imperceptibly during the night, causing the floor to crack. And the cockroaches, which were living underground, came up because they were attracted by the smell of food or by us. It's hard to say which.'

*

The second invasion came on the fifth day. Not cockroaches, this time, but little rodents. When she got up that morning, Laura saw some fifteen of them, tiny little things, pretty even. But they fled out of the french windows to the terrace at high speed as soon as she moved. She found another two in the kitchen, munching bread crumbs. Unlike many other women, Laura was not terrified of mice. Guido summoned the mayor again, drove into Montereale, and came back with two mousetraps, a quarter of a pound of strong cheese, and a red cat, pleasant and patient — so patient, in fact, that he didn't take offence when Bruno tried immediately to gouge out one of his eyes.

'How can this be? First cockroaches climb out of the floor, and now mice,' Livia asked Montalbano, as soon as they'd got into bed.

With Livia lying naked beside him, Montalbano didn't feel like talking about rodents. 'Well, the house hadn't been lived in for a year...' was his vague reply.

'It probably should have been swept, cleaned and disinfected before Laura and her family moved in,' Livia concluded.

'I could do with some of that myself,' Montalbano suggested.

'Some of what?' asked Livia, confused.
'A thorough cleansing.'
And he kissed her.

*

The third invasion came on the eighth day. Again it was Laura, the first to get up, who discovered it. Out of the corner of her eye she saw one, jumped straight into the air and, without knowing how, landed on top of the kitchen table, on her feet, eyes squeezed shut. Then, when she felt it was safe enough, she opened her eyes, trembling and sweaty, and looked at the floor.

Where some thirty spiders were strolling blithely along, as if in a representative parade of the species: one was short and hairy, another had only a ball-like head on very long, wiry legs, a third was reddish and the size of a crab, a fourth was the spitting image of the dreaded black widow . . .

Laura was unfazed by cockroaches and unafraid of mice, but she flew into convulsions the moment she saw a spider. She suffered from 'arachnophobia', a difficult word, which in plain language means an irrational, uncontrollable fear of spiders.

So, with her hair standing on end, she let out an earsplitting scream and fainted, falling off the table and on to the floor, hitting her head, which began to bleed.

Woken with a start, Guido bolted out of bed and rushed to his wife's rescue. But he didn't notice Ruggero

– the cat – racing out of the kitchen, terrorized first by Laura's scream and then by the thud of her fall.

The upshot was that Guido found himself flying parallel to the ground until his head collided, like a bumper, with the fridge.

When Livia arrived at the usual time to go for a swim with her friends, she walked into what looked like a field hospital.

Laura and Guido's heads were wrapped in bandages, while Bruno's foot was taped up: when he'd got out of bed he'd knocked a glass of water off the bedside table. It had shattered on the floor, and he had walked over the slivers of glass. Nonplussed, Livia noticed that even Ruggero was limping – a result of his collision with Guido.

The now familiar squad of pest-controllers arrived, sent by the mayor, who by now had become a friend. With Guido overseeing operations, Laura, who still seemed upset, said to Livia under her breath, 'This house doesn't like us.'

'Oh, come on! A house is a house. It doesn't have likes and dislikes.'

'I'm telling you, it doesn't like us.'

'Oh, please.'

'This house is cursed!' Laura insisted, her eyes sparkling as if she had a fever.

'Please, Laura, don't be silly. I know your nerves are frayed but—'

'I'm beginning to reconsider all those films I've seen about haunted houses full of spirits that come up from hell.'

'But that's all make-believe!'

'I bet I'm right. Just you wait and see.'

*

On the morning of the ninth day, it was raining hard. Livia and Laura went to the Montelusa museum; the major invited Guido to visit a salt mine and he took Bruno with him. That night it rained harder.

*

On the morning of the tenth day, it was still bucketing down. Laura phoned Livia to say she and Guido were taking Bruno to hospital — one of the cuts on his foot was oozing pus. Livia decided to take advantage of the circumstances to put Salvo's house in order. Late that evening the rain stopped, and everyone was convinced that the following day would be clear and hot, perfect for the beach.

TWO

Their prediction proved correct. The sea, no longer grey, had regained its usual colour. The sand, still wet, verged on light brown, but after two hours of sunlight it was gold. The water was perhaps a little cool, but in the heat, which was already intense at seven in the morning, it would be as warm as soup by midday. Which was the temperature Livia liked best. Montalbano couldn't stand it. It made him feel as if he was getting into a hot pool at a spa, and when he came out, he felt sluggish and drained.

Arriving at Pizzo at nine thirty, Livia was pleased to learn that it had been a normal morning so far, with no cockroaches, mice or spiders, or any new arrivals of, say, scorpions or vipers. Laura, Guido and Bruno were ready to go down to the beach.

As they were walking through the little gate on the terrace, they heard the telephone ring in the house. Guido, an engineer with a company that specialized in bridge-building, had been receiving phone calls over the past two days concerning a problem he'd tried to explain to Montalbano with no success. 'You all go on. I'll join you in a minute,' he said. And he went into the house to answer the phone.

'I need to pee,' Laura said to Livia.

She went in too. Livia followed them. Because, for reasons unknown, the need to pee is contagious; all it takes is one person in a crowd needing to pee before everyone has to. She went into the other bathroom.

When each had attended to his or her business, they met once more on the terrace. Guido locked the french windows after they had filed out, closed the little gate behind them, grabbed the beach umbrella — which, being the man, he was obliged to carry — and they headed for the little stone staircase that led down to the beach. Before they began the descent, however, Laura looked around and said, 'Where's Bruno?'

'Maybe he started going down by himself,' said Livia.

'Oh, my God, he can't manage it on his own! I always have to hold his hand!' Laura said, a bit worried.

They leaned out and peered down. From their vantage-point, they could see some twenty or so steps before the staircase turned. No sign of Bruno.

'He can't possibly have got any further,' said Guido.

'Go down and look, for heaven's sake! He may have fallen!' said Laura.

Guido ran down the steps, with Laura and Livia's eyes following him, and disappeared round the turn. Not five minutes later, he reappeared. 'I went to the bottom. He's not there. Go and check the house. We may have locked him in,' he said, in a high voice, panting hard.

'How can we?' said Laura. 'You have the keys!'

Having hoped to spare himself the climb, Guido clambered up, cursing, opened the gate and then the french windows. Then, in chorus, they called, 'Bruno! Bruno!'

'That wretched child is capable of hiding under a bed for the entire day to spite us,' said Guido, who was losing patience.

They searched for him all over the house, under the beds, inside the armoire, on top of the armoire, under the armoire, in the broom cupboard. Nothing. At a certain point, Livia said, 'But there's no sign of Ruggero either.'

It was true. The cat, who was always getting tangled between one's feet — as Guido knew all too well — had disappeared as well.

'Usually he comes when we call him, or at least miaows. Let's try calling him,' Guido suggested.

It was a logical idea, since the child couldn't talk. 'Ruggero! Ruggero!'

No feline response.

'So Bruno must be outside,' Laura surmised.

They went out again and searched, even checking inside the two parked cars. Nothing.

'Bruno! Ruggero! Bruno! Ruggero!'

'Maybe he walked down the track that leads to the main road,' Livia suggested.

Laura's reaction was immediate: 'But if he got that far ... Oh, God, the traffic on that road is awful!'

Guido got into the car and drove slowly down the track, searching left and right. When he reached the end, he turned round and noticed that in front of the rustic cottage there was now a peasant of about fifty, poorly dressed, a dirty beret on his head, staring at the ground so intently that he seemed to be counting the ants.

Guido stopped and stuck his head out of the window. 'Excuse me ...'

'Eh?' said the man, raising his head and batting his eyelids, like someone who had just woken up.

'Have you by any chance seen a little boy pass this way?'

'Who?'

'A three-year-old boy.'

'Why?'

What kind of a question was that? wondered Guido, whose nerves were strained. But he answered, 'Because we can't find him.'

'Ooh, no!' said the fifty-year-old man, looking suddenly concerned and turning three-quarters away, towards his house.

Guido baulked. 'What's that supposed to mean: "Ooh, no"?'

'"Ooh, no" means "ooh, no", no? I never seen this little kid and anyhow I don't know nothing about 'im and I don't want to know nothing 'bout none o' this business,' he said firmly, then went into the house and closed the door behind him.

'Oh, no, you don't! Hey, you!' said Guido, enraged. 'That's no way to talk to people! Where are your manners?'

Spoiling for a fight and needing to let off steam, he got out of the car, went to the door and knocked, even kicked it. But it was hopeless. It remained closed. Cursing, he got back into the car and drove away, past the other house, the one that looked rather better. As it seemed empty, he didn't stop but continued to theirs.

'Nothing?'

'Nothing.'

Laura threw herself into Livia's arms and burst into tears. 'See? Didn't I tell you this house was cursed?'

'Calm down, Laura, for heaven's sake!' her husband shouted.

This only made Laura cry even harder.

'What can we do?' Livia asked.

Guido made up his mind. 'I'm going to ring Emilio.'

'Why the mayor?'

'I'll get him to send the usual squad. Or maybe some policemen. The more of us there are, the better. Don't you think?'

'Wait. Wouldn't it be better to get hold of Salvo?'

'Perhaps you're right.'

*

Twenty minutes later, Montalbano pulled up in a patrol car driven by Gallo, who had raced there as if he was at Monza.

Stepping out of the car, the inspector looked a bit weary, pale and aggrieved, but that was how he always looked after a ride with Gallo.

Livia, Guido and Laura then proceeded to tell him what had happened, all at the same time, so that what little Montalbano was able to understand he grasped only by concentrating hard. Then they stopped and waited for his answer – which was sure to be decisive – with the same expectation as one awaiting grace from Our Lady of Lourdes.

'Could I have a glass of water?' was all he said.

He needed to collect himself, either because of the tremendous heat or to recover from Gallo's prowess behind the wheel. While Guido went to get the water, the two women stared at the inspector in disappointment.

'Where do you think he could be?' asked Livia.

'How should I know, Livia? I'm not a magician! Now, we'll see what we can do. But keep calm, you two. All this agitation distracts me.'

Guido handed him the water, and Montalbano drank

it. 'Could you please tell me what we're doing out here in the sun?' he asked. 'Getting sunstroke? Let's go inside. You too, Gallo.'

Gallo got out of the car and they all obediently followed the inspector.

But, for whatever reason, the minute they were in the living room, Laura's nerves gave way again. First she let out a shrill wail that sounded like the firemen's siren, then started to weep uncontrollably. She'd had a sudden revelation.

'He's been kidnapped!'

'Be reasonable, Laura,' said Guido, trying to bring her to her senses.

'But who would have kidnapped him?' Livia asked.

'How should I know? Gypsies! Albanians! Bedouins! I can *feel* that my poor little boy has been kidnapped!'

Montalbano had a wicked thought. If someone *had* kidnapped a holy terror like Bruno, they would surely give him back by the end of the day. Instead, he asked Laura, 'And why do you think they also kidnapped Ruggero?'

Gallo jumped out of his chair. He knew that one child had disappeared because the inspector had told him so; but after they had arrived at the house he'd remained in the car and hadn't heard anything that the others had told Montalbano. Now it had come out that two were missing? He looked questioningly at his superior.

'Don't worry, he's a cat.'

The idea of the cat had a miraculous effect. Laura

calmed down a little. Montalbano was opening his mouth to say what they needed to do when Livia tensed in her chair, eyes goggling, and said, in a flat voice, 'Oh, my God, oh, my God . . .'

They all turned their eyes in the direction she was looking.

In the living-room doorway sat Ruggero, calm and serene, licking his chops.

Laura let out another siren-like wail and started screaming again. 'Can't you see it's true? The cat's here and Bruno isn't! He's been kidnapped! He's been kidnapped!'

Then she fainted.

Guido and Montalbano picked her up, carried her into the bedroom and laid her on the bed. Livia busied herself making cold compresses for Laura's forehead and held a bottle of vinegar under her nose. No luck. Laura wouldn't open her eyes.

Her face was grey, her jaw clenched, and she was drenched in cold sweat.

'Take her into Montereale to see a doctor,' Montalbano said to Guido. 'You, Livia, go with them.'

Having laid Laura on the back seat with her head on Livia's lap, Guido shot away at a speed that had even Gallo staring in admiration. The inspector and he then went back into the living room.

'Now that they're out of our hair,' Montalbano said to him, 'let's try to do something sensible. And the first sensible thing to do would be to put on our swimming trunks. Otherwise, in this heat, we'll never manage to think clearly.'

'I haven't got mine with me, Chief.'

'Nor have I. But Guido's got three or four pairs.'

They found them and put them on. Luckily they were made of Lycra, since otherwise the inspector would have needed braces and Gallo would have been charged with indecent exposure.

'Now, here's what we'll do. About ten yards past the little gate, there's a stone staircase that leads down to the beach. It's the only place, based on what I could gather from their confused story, where they didn't look closely, I think. I want you to go all the way down, but stopping at every step. The child may have fallen and rolled into some crevice in the rock.'

'And what are you going to do, Chief?'

'I'm going to make friends with the cat.'

Gallo looked at him, dumbfounded, and went out.

'Ruggero!' the inspector called. 'What a beautiful pussy you are! Ruggero!'

The cat rolled on to his back with his paws in the air. Montalbano tickled his belly.

'Prrrrrr . . .' said Ruggero.

'What do you say we go and find out what's in the fridge?' the inspector asked him, heading towards the kitchen.

24

Ruggero, who seemed not to object to the suggestion, followed him, and as Montalbano opened the refrigerator and pulled out two fresh anchovies, the cat rubbed against his legs, butting him lightly.

The inspector pulled out a paper plate, put the anchovies on it, set it on the floor, waited for the cat to finish eating, then went outside onto the terrace. Ruggero, as he'd expected, came after him. He headed for the staircase, in time to see Gallo's head appear.

'Absolutely nothing, Chief. I could swear the kid didn't go down these steps.'

'So, in your opinion, there's no way he could have got down to the beach and into the water?'

'Chief, if I've understood correctly, he's three years old. He couldn't have done it even if he was running.'

'So maybe we ought to do a better search of the surrounding area. There's no other explanation.'

'Chief, why don't we phone the station and ask for some help?' Gallo's sweat was dripping all the way down to his feet.

'Let's wait just a little longer. Meanwhile go and cool off. There's a hose in front of the house.'

'And you should put something on your head. Wait.' Gallo went to the terrace, where various beach accoutrements were scattered, and returned with Livia's hat, which was pink with a floral pattern. 'Here, put this on. Nobody can see you here.'

As Gallo went off, Montalbano noticed Ruggero was no longer with him. He went back into the house, into the kitchen, and called. No cat.

If he wasn't there licking the plate that had held the anchovies, where could he have gone?

From what Laura and Guido had told him, he knew that the cat and the child had become inseparable. Bruno, in fact, had made such a fuss, screaming and crying, that the cat had been allowed to sleep on his bed.

That was why Montalbano had made friends with Ruggero. He had an intuitive sense that the cat knew exactly where the child was. And now, as he stood in the kitchen, it had occurred to him that the cat had disappeared again because he'd gone back to Bruno, to keep him company.

'Gallo!'

Gallo appeared immediately, dripping water all over the floor. 'Your orders, Chief.'

'Listen, look in every room for the cat. With each one, when you're sure he's not there, close the window and door. We have to be sure Ruggero is nowhere in the house, and we have to stop him getting back in.'

Gallo was completely bemused. But weren't they looking for a missing child? Why had the inspector become so fixated on the cat? 'Excuse me, Chief, but what's the animal got to do with it?'

'Just do as I say. Leave only the front door open.'

As Gallo began his search, Montalbano went out

through the little gate, walked to the edge of the cliff, which plunged straight down to the beach, then turned to peer at the house. He studied it long and hard, until he became convinced that what he was seeing was not just an impression. Ever so imperceptibly, by only a few inches, the entire house listed to the left. It must be the result of the ground's having shifted a few days earlier, causing the living-room floor to crack and subsequently releasing the invasions of cockroaches, mice, and spiders.

He went back to the terrace, grabbed a ball that Bruno had left on one of the deck-chairs, and put it on the ground. Slowly, the ball began to roll towards the little wall on the left.

It was the proof he had been looking for. Which might explain everything or nothing.

He went back out through the little gate and walked until he was far enough away to study the right of the house this time. All the windows on that wall were closed, which meant that Gallo had finished on that side. Montalbano saw nothing unusual.

Then he headed behind the house, to the entrance and the parking area. The front door was open, as he'd told Gallo to leave it. Nothing out of the ordinary.

He resumed walking until he could get a good look at the other side, the one where the house listed a little. The tilt was almost invisible. One of the two windows was closed while the other was still open.

'Gallo!'

Gallo's head popped out.

'See anything?'

'This is the smaller bathroom. I've finished. The cat's not here. That leaves only the living room. Can I shut this window?'

As Gallo was closing it, Montalbano noticed that the gutter above it had broken, leaving a gap at least three fingers wide. It must have been an old problem that had never been repaired.

When it rained, the water poured out at that spot instead of going into the pipe that channelled it towards a well at one side of the terrace. To prevent staining on the wall of the house and a gigantic puddle forming on the ground below, somebody had put a big metal drum beneath it, one of those used for storing tar.

Montalbano noticed, however, that the drum had been moved and was no longer perpendicular to the break in the gutter. It now stood at least three feet away from the wall of the house.

If the water could no longer fall straight into the drum, Montalbano reasoned, there should be a great puddle, a lake, since it had rained so hard over the last two days. Instead there was nothing. What was the explanation?

He felt a slight electric shock run down his spine. This usually happened to him when he was on the right track. He went up to the drum. There was, in fact, a little water in it, but not as much as there should have been, and it had certainly fallen in directly from the sky.

At that moment he noticed that the water pouring out of the gap in the gutter for two days and one night had carved a veritable pit at the foot of the wall.

It was impossible to tell immediately why the drum blocked it from view.

The pit had a circumference of about three feet. In all likelihood the surface of friable earth covering some sort of underground cavity had given way under the force of the water falling from above.

Montalbano removed Livia's hat, threw himself flat on the ground, with his face practically inside the pit. Then he moved on to his side and stuck his arm into the opening, without, however, managing to touch the bottom. He realized that the pit did not descend vertically, but slanted, along a sort of gentle incline.

He felt absolutely certain – and couldn't say why – that Bruno had slipped into that pit and couldn't climb out.

He stood up, ran wildly into the house, into the kitchen, opened the refrigerator, grabbed the platter of anchovies, returned to the pit, knelt down and began to place the fish one by one around the entrance.

At that moment Gallo arrived and saw the inspector – who, in the meantime, had put Livia's pink hat back on – sitting on the ground, his chest and arms filthy, staring intently at a hole in the ground ringed with anchovies.

He staggered, feeling at sea, stunned by the suspicion that his superior had lost his mind. What should he do? Humour him, as one does with mad people to keep them calm?

'That's a lovely hole, with all the anchovies round it,' he said, with an admiring smile, as if he was gazing at a work of modern art.

Montalbano gestured imperiously at him to be quiet. Gallo fell silent, afraid that the inspector, in his madness, might turn violent.

THREE

Five minutes later, they were both sitting there motionless. Gallo, too, was staring, spellbound, at the anchovy-adorned pit, having caught the intensity with which Montalbano kept his eye on it. They looked as if sight was their only working sense, as if they'd turned the others off and couldn't hear the breath of the sea or smell the scent of a jasmine near the terrace.

Then, after what seemed an eternity, out of the pit popped the head of Ruggero. He looked at Montalbano, uttered a *mrrrow* of thanks, and attacked the first anchovy.

'Good God!' exclaimed Gallo, having finally understood.

'I'd bet my family jewels,' said Montalbano, standing up, 'that the child is down there.'

'Let's find a shovel!'

'Don't be an idiot. The ground's so soft, it'd cave in.'

'What shall we do?'

'You stay here and watch what the cat does. I'm going to ring Fazio from the car.'

＊

'Fazio?'

'At your service, Chief.'

'Listen, I'm with Gallo in the Pizzo district, at Montereale Marina.'

'I know the place.'

'There's a little boy, the son of some friends, who I think has fallen into a deep pit in the ground and can't get out.'

'I'll come over straight away.'

'No. Call the fire chief at Montelusa. This is their sort of thing. Tell him the ground is very friable, and they should bring proper tools for digging and shoring up the walls. And, most importantly, no sirens, no noise. I don't want the media finding out – heaven forbid that this should turn into another Vermicino.'

'Shall I come too?'

'There's no need.'

He went into the house and called Livia's mobile from the telephone in the living room. 'How's Laura doing?'

'She's asleep. They gave her a sedative. We were just getting into the car. Any news on Bruno?'

'I think I know where he is.'

'Oh, God! What does that mean?'

'It means he fell into a hole and can't get out.'

'But ... is he alive?'

'I don't know. I hope so. The firemen will be here soon. When the hospital discharges Laura, take her to our place in Marinella. I don't want her here. Guido can come, if he wants.'

'Keep me informed. I mean it.'

*

He went back to Gallo, who hadn't moved. 'What did the cat do?'

'He ate all the anchovies and went into the house. Didn't you see him?'

'No. He must have gone into the kitchen for a drink.'

Montalbano had noticed some time ago that his hearing wasn't as good as it had once been. Nothing serious, but its clarity, like clarity of vision, had dulled. His ears used to be so keen he could hear the grass growing. Damned age! 'How's your hearing?' he asked Gallo.

'I've got sharp ears, Chief.'

'See if you can hear anything.'

Gallo lay flat on the ground, belly down, and stuck his head into the pit.

'I think I heard something.' He covered his ears with his hands, took a deep breath, lowered his hands, then stuck his head back into the pit. Less than a minute later, he raised it and turned to Montalbano wearing an expression of content. 'I heard him crying. I'm sure of it. He may've hurt himself when he fell. But it sounded really, really far away. How deep is this pit?'

'Well, injured or not, at least we know he's alive. And that's very good news.'

At that moment Ruggero reappeared, said *mrrrow*, hopped blithely into the hole and disappeared.

'He's gone to visit Bruno,' said the inspector.

Gallo made as if to get up, but Montalbano held him back. 'Wait a minute,' he said. 'Can you still hear the kid crying?'

Gallo listened for a long time, then said, 'No.'

'You see? Having Ruggero there comforts him.'

'What do we do now?'

'I'm going into the kitchen to get myself a beer. You want one?'

'Nah. I'll have an orangeade. I saw some in the fridge.'

They felt satisfied, even though a long and difficult road lay ahead of them, trying to pull the little boy out of the hole.

*

Montalbano drank his beer slowly, then rang Livia. 'He's alive.' He told her the whole story.

When he'd finished, Livia asked, 'Should I tell Laura?'

'Well, it won't be easy to pull him out, and the

firemen haven't arrived. You'd better not say anything yet. Is Guido still with you?'

'No. He drove us to Marinella and now he's on his way back to you.'

*

One could tell immediately that the captain of the six-man squad of firefighters knew how to do his job. Montalbano explained what he thought had happened, mentioned the shift in the ground that had occurred several days earlier, and told him of his impression that the house was listing.

The captain pulled out a spirit-level and a plumb-line and checked. 'You're right,' he said.

Then he got down to work. First he tested the ground around the house with a kind of steel-tipped stick, then he looked inside the house, stopping to examine the cemented-up crack in the living-room floor through which the cockroaches had entered, then came back out. He stuck a flexible metal tape-measure into the pit, let it play out a long way, then rewound it, stuck it back in, then rewound it again. He was trying to find out how deep it might be.

'There's an inclined plane in there,' he said, after doing some mathematical calculations, 'which begins almost directly under the smaller bathroom window and ends under the bedroom window, about twenty feet down.'

'You mean the depression runs the full length of this side of the house?' asked Guido.

'Exactly,' said the fire chief. 'Which is a very strange path for it to follow.'

'Why?' asked Montalbano.

'Because if the depression was caused by rainwater, that means something underneath diminished the water's force of penetration, preventing it spreading entirely through the ground and being for the most part reabsorbed. The water came up against an obstacle, a solid barrier, which forced it to follow an inclined plain.'

'Can you handle it?'

'We must proceed with extreme caution,' was the fire chief's reply. 'The soil surrounding the house is different from the rest and the slightest movement could make it give way.'

'What do you mean, "different from the rest"?' asked Montalbano.

'Follow me,' the fire chief said.

He took some ten steps away from the house, with Montalbano and Guido following.

'Look at the colour of the soil here, then look how, ten yards ahead, near the house, it changes. The soil we're standing on is natural to this place. That other soil, which is lighter and yellowish, is sandy. It was brought here.'

'Why did they do that?'

'I have no idea,' said the fire chief. 'Maybe to make

the house stand out, make it look more elegant. Ah, at last, here's the mechanical shovel.'

*

Before he put the excavator to work, though, the fire chief wanted to lighten the weight of the sandy soil lying over the path of the depression. So, shovels in hand, three firemen began to dig along the side of the house, dumping the earth into three wheelbarrows, which their colleagues emptied about ten yards away.

After they had removed about a foot of soil, they had a surprise. At the point where the house's foundations should have begun, there was a second wall, perfectly plastered. To protect the plaster from damp, sheets of plastic had been stuck over the wall.

In short, it was as if the house continued, wrapped up, underground.

'All of you, dig under the window of the little bathroom,' the fire chief ordered.

Little by little, the upper part of another window, perfectly aligned with the one above, began to emerge. It had no frame, but was only a rectangular aperture with double sheets of plastic over it.

'There's another apartment down here!' said Guido, in astonishment.

At this point, Montalbano understood everything. 'Stop digging!' he ordered.

Everyone stopped and looked at him questioningly.

'Has anyone got a torch?' he asked.

'I'll fetch one!' said a firefighter.

'Break the plastic covering the window,' the inspector ordered.

Two jabs of the shovel sufficed. The firemen brought him the torch.

'Wait here,' Montalbano said, straddling the window-sill.

He no longer needed the torch, since the light coming in through the window was more than enough for him to see by. He found himself inside a small bathroom, identical with the one on the floor above it. It was, moreover, perfectly finished, with tiled floors and walls, a shower, washbasin, lavatory and bidet.

As he was wondering what this might mean, something grazed his leg, making him jump.

'*Mrrrow,*' said Ruggero.

'Nice to see you again,' said the inspector.

He turned on the torch and followed the cat into the room next door.

There, the weight of the water and soil had broken through the plastic over the window, turning the room into a bog.

Bruno was standing in a corner, eyes shut tight. He had a cut on his forehead and was trembling all over as if he had a fever.

'Bruno, it's me, Salvo,' the inspector said softly.

The little boy opened his eyes, recognized Montalbano, and ran to him, open-armed. The inspector embraced him, and Bruno started to cry.

At that moment Guido, who couldn't wait any longer, burst into the room.

*

'Livia? Bruno's all right.'

'Is he injured?'

'He has a cut on his forehead, but I don't think it's serious. Guido is taking him to A and E in Montereale. Tell Laura and, if it's all right with her, take her there. I'll wait for you all here.'

*

The fire chief struggled out of the window through which Montalbano had entered. He looked bewildered. 'There's a whole apartment down here, exactly like the one upstairs. There's even a terrace with a railing around it! All you'd have to do is install the internal and external window frames, which are stacked in the living room, and you could move in! There's even running water — and the electrical system is all ready to be hooked up to the mains. What I don't understand is why they buried it underground.'

Montalbano, for his part, had a precise idea of why they'd done it. 'I think I do. I'm sure that originally they'd been granted a building permit for a bungalow. But the owner, in league with the builder and the work foreman, had the house built as we see it. Then he had the ground floor covered with sandy soil, so that only the upstairs remained visible, turning it into the ground floor.'

'Yes, but why did he do it?'

'He was waiting for an amnesty on code violations. The moment the government approved it, he would remove the earth covering the other apartment, then put in his request for amnesty. Otherwise he risked having the whole house demolished, even though that's unlikely around here.'

The fire chief was laughing. 'Demolished? Around here whole towns have been built illegally!'

'Yes, but I found out that the owner lived in Germany. It's possible he forgot about our wonderful ancient customs and thought that people respected the law here as they do in Cologne.'

The fire chief seemed unconvinced. 'Okay – but this government has granted amnesty after amnesty. Why, then—'

'He died a few years ago.'

'What should we do? Put everything back as it was?'

'No, leave it. Could that create any problems?'

'For the upstairs, you mean? No, none whatsoever.'

'I want to show this fine handiwork to the owner of the agency that let the house.'

*

Left alone, the inspector had a shower, dried himself in the sun, then got dressed. He grabbed another bottle of beer. He had worked up a serious appetite. What was taking the gang so long?

'Hello, Livia? Are you still in A and E?'

'No, we're on our way. Bruno's fine.'

He hung up and dialled Enzo's trattoria. 'Montalbano here. I know it's late and you're about to close, but if I came in with a party of four plus a child, could we have something to eat?'

'For you, Inspector, we're always open.'

*

As always happens, the narrow escape had made everyone so giddy and ravenous that Enzo, hearing them laughing and eating non-stop as if they'd just broken a week-long fast, asked what they were celebrating. Bruno behaved as if he'd been bitten by a tarantula, jumping about, knocking the cutlery off the table, then a glass that luckily didn't break and, last, spilling the olive oil over Montalbano's trousers. For a brief moment the inspector regretted having been so quick to pull him out of the hole, then felt guilty for having thought such a thing.

When everyone had finished eating, Livia and her friends drove back to Pizzo. Montalbano raced home to change his trousers, then went to the office to work.

*

ANDREA CAMILLERI

That evening, he asked Fazio if a patrol car was available to take him home.

'There's Gallo, Chief.'

'Nobody else?' He wanted to avoid another Monza-style dash like the one he'd endured that morning.

'No, sir.'

Once in the car, he admonished Gallo, 'We're in no hurry this time. Drive slowly.'

'Tell me how fast you want me to go, Chief.'

'Twenty miles per hour, max.'

'Twenty? Chief, I don't even *know* how to drive at twenty miles an hour. I'm liable to crash into something. What do you say we go thirty-five, forty?'

'Okay.'

Everything went smoothly until they turned off the main road and onto the track leading to the house. In front of the rustic cottage, a dog ran in front of them. To avoid it, Gallo swerved and nearly crashed into the front door, shattering an earthenware jug beside it.

'You've broken something,' said Montalbano.

As they were getting out of the car, the cottage door opened and a peasant of about fifty appeared, wearing shabby clothes and a dirty beret.

'What happened?' asked the man, turning on the small light over the door.

'We broke your jug and wanted to compensate you for the damage,' said Gallo, in perfect Italian.

Then something strange happened. The man looked

42

at the patrol car, turned round, extinguished the light, went back into the cottage and locked the door. Gallo looked puzzled.

'He saw the police car,' said Montalbano. 'Apparently he doesn't like us. Try knocking.'

Gallo knocked. Nobody came to the door.

'Hey! Is anyone at home?'

Nobody answered.

'Let's get out of here,' said the inspector.

*

Laura and Livia had laid the table on the terrace. The evening was so beautiful it was heartbreaking. The heat of the day had mysteriously given way to a restorative cool, and the moon floating over the sea was so bright that they could have eaten by its light alone.

The two women had prepared a simple meal, since they'd gone late to Enzo's where they had stuffed themselves.

As they were sitting round the table, Guido told the others what had transpired that morning between himself and the peasant from the rustic cottage.

'As soon as I said a little boy had disappeared, he said, "Ooh no," and ran and shut himself up in the house. I knocked and knocked, but he wouldn't open the door.'

So it's not just the police he has problems with, thought the inspector. But he didn't say anything about the nearly identical treatment he had received.

After they'd eaten, Guido and Laura suggested everyone go for a walk on the beach in the moonlight. Livia declined, and so did Montalbano. Luckily, Bruno chose to go with his parents.

After they'd been sitting for a while in the deck-chairs, enjoying a silence broken only by the purring of Ruggero, who was luxuriating on the inspector's lap, Livia said, 'Would you take me to where you found Bruno? Since we've been back, Laura has forbidden me to go and look at it.'

'All right. Let me fetch a torch. There's one in the car.'

'Guido must have one somewhere. I'll see if I can find it.'

They met in front of the excavated window, each with a torch in hand. Montalbano climbed over the sill first, checked to make sure there weren't any rats, then helped Livia inside. Naturally, Ruggero hopped in after them.

'Unbelievable!' said Livia, gazing at the bathroom.

The air was damp and heavy. The only window through which any clean air could enter was not enough to ventilate the space. They went into the room where the inspector had found Bruno.

'You'd better not go any further, Livia. It's a swamp.'

'The poor child! He must have been so scared!' said Livia, heading for the living room.

In the torch beams they saw the window frames, wrapped in plastic. Montalbano noticed a rather large trunk pushed up against a wall. Overcome with curiosity – since it wasn't locked – he opened it.

At that moment he looked exactly like Cary Grant in *Arsenic and Old Lace*. He slammed the lid shut and sat on top of it. When the beam from Livia's torch shone on his face, he smiled automatically.

'What are you smiling about?'

'Me? I'm not smiling.'

'So why are you making that face?'

'What face?'

'What's in the trunk?' Livia asked.

'Nothing. It's empty.'

How could he possibly have told her there was a corpse inside?

FOUR

When Guido and Laura returned from their romantic stroll along the moonlit beach, it was past eleven. 'That was amazing!' Laura exclaimed enthusiastically. 'I really needed that after a day like today.'

Guido was a little less enthusiastic, given that halfway through their walk, Bruno had suddenly become very sleepy, and he'd had to carry him the rest of the way.

Ever since he'd sat down in the deck-chair after his visit to the phantom apartment with Livia, Montalbano had been beset by a dilemma worse than Hamlet's: to tell or not to tell? If he told them there was an unidentified corpse downstairs, indescribable chaos would break out and the rest of the night would be hell, or almost. It was more than certain, in fact, that Laura would adamantly refuse to spend one minute more under that roof and demand to sleep somewhere else.

But where? At Marinella there wasn't even a guest room. They would have to camp out. And how would they do that? He imagined how they would work things out, with Laura, Livia and Bruno in the double bed, Guido on the sofa, and himself in the armchair. He shuddered.

No, that was no solution. Better a hotel. But where, at midnight, in Vigàta, would they find one that was still open? Maybe Montelusa was a better bet. Which would mean phone call after phone call, back and forth in the car to and from Montelusa to keep their friends company and, as icing on the cake, the inevitable all-night argument with Livia.

'But why did you have to choose *that* house?'

'Livia darling, how was I to know there was a dead body in it?'

'How were you to know? What kind of policeman are you, anyway?'

No, he decided, it was better, for now, to say nothing to anyone.

After all, God only knew how long the corpse had been in the trunk. One day more or one day less wasn't going to make any difference. Nor would it affect the investigation.

Having said goodbye to their friends, then, Livia and the inspector headed back to Marinella.

The moment Livia went for a shower, Montalbano, from the terrace, called Fazio on his mobile phone, keeping his voice down. 'Fazio? Montalbano here.'

'What's wrong, Chief?'

'I haven't time to explain. In ten minutes I want you

to call me at home and say you need me urgently at the station.'

'Why? What's happened?'

'Don't ask questions. Just do as I say.'

'And what do I do afterwards?'

'You hang up and go back to sleep.'

Five minutes later Livia emerged from the bathroom and Montalbano went in. As he was brushing his teeth, he heard the phone ring. As expected, Livia went to pick it up. This would make the scene he had staged more credible.

'Salvo, Fazio's on the phone!'

He went into the dining room with his toothbrush still in his mouth, lips frothing with paste, muttering to himself for Livia's benefit as she glared at him: 'Can't I ever have a little peace and quiet, even at this hour?' He grabbed the phone and said gruffly, 'What is it?'

'You're needed at the station.'

'Can't you guys handle it? ... No? Okay, okay, I'll be right there.'

He slammed down the receiver, feigning anger. 'Won't they ever grow up? Why do they always need Daddy's help? I'm sorry, Livia, but, unfortunately I—'

'I understand,' said Livia, in a tone straight from the polar ice-caps. 'I'm going to bed.'

'Will you wait up for me?'

'No.'

He got dressed, went outside, got into the car and

headed for Marina di Montereale. He drove extremely slowly: he wanted to waste as much time as possible, to be more or less certain that Laura and Guido had gone to bed.

When he got to Pizzo, he went as far as the second house — the uninhabited but well-maintained one — stopped and got out with his torch. He travelled the remaining stretch of the track on foot, afraid that if he came any closer with the car, the sound, in the night's stillness, might wake his friends.

No light shone in any of the windows, a good sign that Laura and Guido were well on their way to Dreamland.

With a light step he sidled up to the window that served as a door, climbed over the sill and went in. Then he turned on the torch and moved towards the living room.

He lifted the trunk's lid. The corpse was barely visible, having been wrapped several times in the same sheets of plastic that had been used to seal off the secret apartment, then bound in brown packing tape wound many times around the bundle. It looked like a cross between a mummy and a giant parcel ready for shipping.

He shone the torch closer and realized, from what he could see, that the body was fairly well preserved. Apparently the plastic had created a vacuum, not allowing even a trace of the terrible stench of death to leak out. Forcing himself to look harder, he noticed a great deal of long blonde hair on and around the head. The face, on the other hand, he couldn't make out, because it had been wrapped twice with the brown tape.

It was a woman, that much was clear.

There was nothing more to see or do. He closed the trunk, left the apartment, walked back to his car, and drove home.

He found Livia in bed but still awake. She was reading a book. 'Darling, I got back as quickly as I could. I'll just have the shower I wasn't able to—'

'Go on, hurry. Don't waste any more time.'

✻

When Livia came out of the bathroom at nine o'clock the following morning, she found Montalbano on the veranda.

'What? Are you still here? You told me you had to go to the station to deal with that business of last night.'

'I've changed my mind. I'm going to take half a day's holiday. I'm coming with you to Pizzo to spend the morning with you and your friends.'

'Oh, goody!'

By the time they got there Laura, Guido and Bruno were ready to go down to the beach. Since they had decided to spend the whole day outside, Laura had filled some baskets with food.

But how and when – the inspector wondered anxiously

in the meantime — should he break the good news to them?

It was Guido who helped him out. 'Did you phone the people at the agency to tell them about the illegal apartment?'

'Not yet.'

'Why not?'

'Because I'm afraid they might raise your rent, since you now have another apartment at your disposal.'

He was trying to make a joke of it, but Livia intervened: 'Come on, what are you waiting for? I want to see the look on the face of the guy who let it to you.'

And I can't wait to see yours in a few minutes! thought Montalbano. But he said, 'Well, there's a major complication.'

'What?'

'Could you send Bruno away for a minute?' Montalbano asked Laura under his breath.

She gave him a puzzled look, but did as he said. 'Bruno, will you do Mummy a little favour? Go into the kitchen and fetch another bottle of mineral water from the fridge.'

The others stared at him, their curiosity aroused by his question.

'So?'

When Bruno had gone, he said, 'The fact is, I found a dead body. A woman's.'

'Where?' Guido asked.

'In the apartment downstairs. In the living room. Inside a trunk.'

'Are you joking?' asked Laura.

'No, he's not,' said Livia. 'I know him well. Did you discover it last night when we went down there?'

Bruno returned with a bottle.

'Go and get another!' they said in unison.

The child set the bottle on the floor and ran off.

'And you,' said Livia, who was beginning to understand what was happening, 'let my friends spend the night here with a dead body in the house?'

'Come on, Livia! It's downstairs! It's not contagious!'

All of a sudden Laura let out the siren wail that had become her speciality.

Ruggero, who had been sunning himself atop the terrace wall, high-tailed away. Bruno returned, put the second bottle on the floor and ran to get another without anyone having asked him.

'You bastard!' Guido said angrily, and followed his wife, who had run weeping into the bedroom.

'But I did what I thought was best!' said Montalbano, trying to justify himself in Livia's eyes.

She stared at him disdainfully. 'When Fazio phoned you last night, you had already arranged with him to provide you with an excuse to go out, hadn't you?'

'Yes.'

'And did you come back here to have a better look at the corpse?'

'Yes.'

'And afterwards you made love to me! You're an animal! A brute!'

'But I had a shower so that—'

'You're repulsive!'

She got up, leaving him standing there, and went into her friends' bedroom. She returned about five minutes later, cold as ice. 'They're packing their bags.'

'What about the plane tickets?'

'Guido decided not to stay any longer. They'll drive. Take me back to Marinella. I need to pack, too, because I'm going with them.'

'Oh, Livia, be reasonable!'

'I don't want to hear another word!'

It was hopeless. On the drive back to Marinella, she didn't open her mouth and Montalbano didn't dare. As soon as they arrived, Livia threw her things helter-skelter into her suitcase, then went out and sat on the veranda with a long face.

'Would you like me to make you something to eat?'

'You only ever think of two things.'

She didn't say what those two things were, but Montalbano understood what she'd meant.

Around one o'clock, Guido arrived to pick up Livia. Also in the car was Ruggero, with whom Bruno had apparently refused to part. Guido handed the house keys to Montalbano, but did not shake his hand. Laura kept her head turned away, Bruno blew him a raspberry, and Livia wouldn't even kiss him goodbye.

Rejected and abandoned, Montalbano watched them leave with a heavy heart. But also, deep down, a sense of relief.

*

The first thing he did was phone Adelina.

'Adelì, Livia had to go back to Genoa. Can you come tomorrow morning?'

'Yes, Signore. I could come in a couple of hours if you like.'

'That's all right, there's no need.'

'No, Signore, I'ma going to come anyways. I can just imagina mess Miss Livia lefta house in!'

There was a little bit of hard bread in the kitchen. Montalbano ate it with a slice of *tumazzo* cheese he found in the fridge. Then he went to bed and fell asleep.

When he woke up it was four o'clock. He could hear, from the tinkle of plates and glasses in the kitchen, that Adelina had already arrived. 'Could you bring me a cup of coffee, Adelì?'

'Straight away, Signore.'

When she brought the coffee she was scowling. '*Madonna mia!* The plates was all covered with grease an' I even foun' a pair o' dirty unnerpants in the bat'room!'

Now, in reality, if there was a fanatically neat woman in the world it was Livia. But in Adelina's eyes, she had always seemed like someone whose ideal was to live in a pigsty.

'But I told you she had to leave in a hurry.'

'You have a fight? You break up?'

'No, we didn't.'

Adelina seemed disappointed and went back to the kitchen.

Montalbano got up to make a phone call. 'Aurora estate agency? Inspector Montalbano here. I'd like to speak with Mr Callara.'

'Trying to connect you,' replied a woman's voice.

'Inspector? Good afternoon, what can I do for you?'

'Are you in the office for the day?'

'Yes, I'll be here till we close. Why?'

'I'll be around in half an hour to return the keys to the beach house.'

'What? Weren't they supposed to stay until—'

'Yes, but my friends were forced to leave this morning. A sudden death.'

'Listen, Inspector, I don't know if you read the contract . . .'

'I glanced at it. Why?'

'Because it states clearly that the client gets nothing back in the event of an early departure.'

'Did I ask for anything back, Mr Callara?'

'Ah, okay. Well, then, don't bother coming here

yourself. I'll send someone down to the station to pick up the keys.'

'I need to talk to you and then show you something.'

'Come whenever you like.'

*

'Catarella? Montalbano here.'

'I already rec'nized ya in as much as yer voice is all yours, Chief.'

'Any news?'

'No, sir, Chief, nuttin'. 'Xcept fer Filippo Ragusano – you know him, Chief, he's a one wherats is got a shoe store by the church, and 'e shot 'is brother-'n-law Gasparino Manzella.'

'Did he kill him?'

'Nossir, Chief, jes' grazed 'im.'

'Why did he shoot him?'

'Says Gasparino Manzanella was gettin on 'is noives since it was rilly hot 'n' all an' a fly was walkin' on 'is 'ead, which rilly bugged 'im an' so 'e shot 'im.'

'Fazio there?'

'Nossir, Chief. 'E went out by the iron bridge 'cause some guy busted 'is wife's 'ead out that way.'

'Okay. I wanted to tell you—'

'But there's somethin' else happened.'

'Oh, yes? I was somehow under the impression that nothing had. What did?'

'What happened izzat Corporeal 'Tective Alberto

Virduzzo went into a muddy locality and slipped wit' both 'is legs in the mud that was there, breakin' one o' the legs aforesaid. Gallo took 'im to the hospitable.'

'Listen, I wanted to tell you that I'll be late coming in.'

'You're the boss, Chief.'

*

Mr Callara was busy with a client. Montalbano stepped outside to smoke a cigarette in the open air. It was so hot that the asphalt was melting; his shoes stuck to it. Once Callara was free, he came out to meet Montalbano. 'Please come into my office, Inspector. I've got air-conditioning.'

Which Montalbano hated. Never mind.

'Before I take you to see something—'

'Where do you want to take me?'

'To the house you let to my friends.'

'Why? Is anything wrong? Something broken?'

'No, everything's fine. But I think you should come.'

'As you wish.'

'I believe I remember you saying, when you took me to see the house, that a man who had emigrated to Germany had built it. A certain Angelo Speciale, who had married a German widow, whose son – Ralf, I think you said – had come here with his stepfather, then mysteriously disappeared on their way back to Germany. Is that correct?'

Callara looked at him in admiration. 'Absolutely. What a memory you've got!'

'You, naturally, will have the name, address and telephone number of Mrs Speciale?'

'Of course. Wait a minute while I look for the information on Mrs Gudrun.'

Montalbano wrote it down on a scrap of paper. Callara became curious.

'For what purpose—'

'You'll understand later. I seem also to remember that you gave me the name of the developer who designed the house and oversaw the construction.'

'Yes. His name is Michele Spitaleri. Would you like his phone number?'

'Yes.' Montalbano jotted that down, too.

'Listen, Inspector. Can't you tell me why—'

'I'll tell you on the way there. Here's the key. Keep it with you.'

'Will this take long?'

'I couldn't say.'

Callara gave him an inquisitive look. Montalbano donned an expressionless mask.

'Maybe I'd better tell my secretary,' said Callara.

*

They set off in Montalbano's car. On the way, the inspector told Callara how little Bruno had disappeared, how hard it had been to find him and, finally, how they'd pulled him out with the help of the firemen.

Callara was worried about one thing only: 'Did they do any damage?'

'Who?'

'The firemen. Did they damage the house in any way?'

'No, not inside.'

'That's a relief. 'Cause once when a fire broke out in the kitchen of a house I'd let, they did more damage than the fire.'

Not a word about the illegal apartment.

'Do you intend to inform Mrs Gudrun?'

'Of course, of course. But she certainly doesn't know anything about this. It must have been an idea of Angelo Speciale's. I'll have to deal with everything myself.'

'Are you going to apply for amnesty?'

'Well, I don't know if—'

'Mr Callara, don't forget that I'm a public official. I can't just look the other way.'

'What if — just supposing, mind you — what if I inform Spitaleri and have everything put back as it—'

'Then I will charge you, Mrs Gudrun and Spitaleri with illegal construction.'

'Well, if that's how it is . . .'

✳

'Look at that! Look at it!' was Mr Callara's exclamation of wonderment as he entered through the bathroom window and saw it ready for use.

Torch in hand, Montalbano led him into the other rooms.

'Look at that! Look at it!'

They arrived in the living room.

'Look at that! Look at it!'

'See?' said Montalbano. 'Even the window frames are ready for installation.'

'Look at that! Look at it!'

As if by chance, the inspector let the torch beam fall upon the trunk.

'And what's that?' asked Callara.

'It looks like a trunk to me.'

'What's inside? Have you opened it?'

'Me? No. Why would I do that?'

'Would you lend me the torch a minute?'

'Here.' Everything was going as planned.

Callara opened the trunk, and when he aimed the beam inside, he did not say, 'Look at that,' but took a great leap backwards. 'Ohmygod! Ohmygod!'

The torch beam trembled in his hand.

'What is it?'

'But ... but ... there's a ... there's a ... dead person!'

'Really?'

FIVE

Thus, with the dead body's deadness now official, the inspector could look into doing something about it. First, however, he had to do something about Signor Callara, who, having dashed out through the window, was now vomiting even what he had eaten the week before.

Montalbano opened the apartment upstairs, made Mr Callara, who was feeling very dizzy, lie down on the sofa in the living room and went to fetch him a glass of water.

'Can I go home?'

'You must be joking. I can't drive you.'

'I'll call my son and ask him to come and get me.'

'Not on your life! You have to wait for the public prosecutor! It was you who discovered the body, no? Would you like a little more water?'

'No, I feel cold.'

Cold? In this heat?

'I've got a blanket in the car. I'll fetch it.'

His role as Good Samaritan over, he called the station. 'Catarella? Is Fazio there?'

'He'll be coming soon.'

'What does that mean?'

'He phoned just now sayin' zackly, "I'll be there in five minutes." What I mean is, *he* will be here in five minutes, not me, since I'm already here.'

'Listen, a dead body's been found, and I want him to call me at this number.' He gave him the telephone number of the house.

'Hee, hee!' said Catarella.

'Are you laughing or crying?'

'Laughin', Chief.'

'Why's that?'

''Cause normalwise iss always me tellin' you when summon finds a dead body an' now iss you tellin' me!'

*

Five minutes later, the telephone rang.

'What is it, Chief? You find a dead body?'

'The head of the agency that let the apartment to my friends found it. Luckily they'd already left before this wonderful discovery was made.'

'Recently killed?'

'I don't think so. In fact, I'd rule that out. But I didn't get a good look at it, because I had to give a hand to Mr Callara, poor man.'

'So, it's the same house where I sent the firemen?'

'Exactly. Marina di Montereale, Pizzo district, the house at the end of the unmade road. Bring some back-up. And inform the prosecutor, Forensics, and Dr Pasquano. I don't feel like doing it myself.'

'I'll be with you as soon as I can, Chief.'

*

As he was putting on his gloves, Fazio, who'd come with Galluzzo, asked Montalbano, 'Can I go down and have a look?'

The inspector was reclining in a deck-chair on the terrace, enjoying the sunset. 'Of course. Be careful not to leave any fingerprints.'

'You're not coming?'

'What for?'

*

Half an hour later, the usual pandemonium broke out.

First the Forensics team arrived, but since they couldn't see a damn thing in the underground living room, they lost another half-hour setting up a temporary electrical connection.

Then Pasquano arrived, with the ambulance and his team of undertakers. Realizing immediately that he would have to wait his turn, he pulled up a deck-chair, sat down beside the inspector and dozed off.

An hour or so later, by which time the sun had almost set, someone from Forensics came and woke him.

'Doctor,' he said, 'the body's wrapped up. What should we do?'

'Unwrap it,' was the laconic reply.

'Yes, but who should do the unwrapping? Us or you?'

'I suppose I'd better unwrap it myself,' said Pasquano, with a sigh.

'Fazio!' Montalbano called.

'Chief?'

'Has Prosecutor Tommaseo arrived yet?'

'No, Chief. He rang to say it would take him at least an hour to get here.'

'You know what I'm going to do?'

'No, sir.'

'I'm going out to eat. It looks to me as if things are going to take a long time.' Passing through the living room, he noticed that Callara hadn't moved from the sofa. He took pity on him. 'Come with me, I'll give you a lift to Vigàta. I'll tell the prosecutor how things went.'

'Oh, thank you, thank you,' said Callara, and handed him the blanket.

*

He dropped Callara off in front of his agency, which was now closed.

'Don't forget. Not a word to anyone about the corpse you found.'

'My dear inspector, I think I'm running a fever of a

hundred and two. I don't even feel like breathing, let alone talking.'

Since going to Enzo's would take too long, he drove back to Marinella instead.

In the fridge he found a rather sizeable platter of *caponata* and a big piece of Ragusan *caciocavallo* cheese. Adelina had even bought him some fresh bread. He was so hungry, his eyes were burning.

It took him a good hour to polish it all off, to the accompaniment of half a litre of wine. Then he washed his face, got into his car and drove back to Pizzo.

*

The moment the inspector arrived Tommaseo, the public prosecutor, who'd been standing in the parking area in front of the house getting a breath of air, came running up to him. 'It looks like a sex-related crime!'

His eyes were sparkling, his tone almost festive. That was how Prosecutor Tommaseo was: any crime of passion, any killing related to infidelity or sex, was pure bliss to him. Montalbano was convinced he was a maniac, but only in his mind.

Tommaseo would drool over every woman he interrogated, yet nobody knew of any female friends or lovers in his life.

'Is Dr Pasquano still here?' asked Montalbano.

'Yes.'

It was stifling in the illegal apartment. Too many

people going in and out, too much heat given off by the two floodlights the Forensics team had turned on. The already close atmosphere was a lot more so, with the difference that now it stank of men's sweat and also the stench of death.

The corpse had been taken out of the trunk and unwrapped as far as possible: pieces of the plastic were still sticking to the skin, perhaps having fused with it over time. The men had placed the body on the stretcher as naked as they'd found it, and Dr Pasquano, cursing under his breath, was finishing his examination. Montalbano realized it wasn't a good time to ask him anything.

'Get me the prosecutor!' the doctor ordered.

Tommaseo came in.

'Listen, Judge, I can't go on working in here. It's too hot, the thing's liquefying before my eyes. Can I take it away?'

Tommaseo looked enquiringly at the head of Forensics, Vanni Arquà.

'If you're asking me, yes,' said Arquà.

Arquà and Montalbano got on each other's nerves. They didn't say hello when they met, and only spoke to one another when strictly necessary.

'Okay, take the body out and put seals over the window,' Tommaseo ordered.

Pasquano glanced at Montalbano. Without saying anything to anyone, the inspector went back upstairs, took a bottle of beer from the fridge – Guido had restocked it

— and returned to the terrace where he settled into the same deck-chair. He heard cars leaving.

A few minutes later Dr Pasquano appeared, and sat down as before. 'I see you know the house well. Could I have a beer too?'

When the inspector was on his way to the kitchen, Fazio and Galluzzo came in.

'Chief, can we go now?'

'Sure. Take this piece of paper. It's the phone number of a developer named Michele Spitaleri. I want you to track him down immediately. You absolutely must find him and tell him I'll be waiting for him at the station tomorrow morning, nine o'clock sharp. Good night.'

He took the cold beer out to Pasquano and told him how and why he knew the house so well. Then he said, 'Doctor, it's too beautiful an evening for me to piss you off. Tell me if you want to answer a few of my questions or not.'

'No more than four or five.'

'Did you manage to determine her age?'

'Yes. She was probably fifteen or sixteen. That's one.'

'Tommaseo told me it was a sex-related crime.'

'Tommaseo is a perverted idiot. That's two.'

'What do you mean? You can't count that as a question! Don't cheat! We're still on the first!'

'Oh, all right.'

'Second question: was she raped?'

'I'm not in a position to say. Maybe not even after the post-mortem. Although I would assume she was.'

'Third: how was she killed?'

'They cut her throat.'

'Four: how long ago?'

'Five or six years. She was well preserved because they'd wrapped her up well.'

'Five: in your opinion, was she killed down there or somewhere else?'

'You should ask Forensics. Whatever the case, Arquà found plenty of traces of blood on the floor.'

'Six—'

'No, no, no! Time's up and the beer's finished. Good night.'

He got up and left. Montalbano also stood up, but only to fetch himself another beer from the kitchen.

He couldn't bear to leave the terrace on a night like this. All of a sudden he missed Livia. Just the previous evening they'd been sitting in exactly the same place, in harmony and in love.

Suddenly the night felt cold.

*

Fazio was at the station by eight o'clock the next morning. Montalbano arrived half an hour later.

'Chief, you've got to forgive me, but I just don't believe it.'

'You just don't believe what?'

'The story of how the body was discovered.'

'How else was it supposed to have been discovered,

Fazio? Callara happened to see the trunk, he lifted the lid and—'

'Chief, if you ask me, you arranged things so that Callara would be the one to open it.'

'Why would I do that?'

'Because you'd already found the body the day before, when you went to get the child. You've got a nose like a hunting dog's, Chief. As if you weren't going to open that trunk! And you didn't say anything so your friends could leave in peace.'

He'd understood everything. It wasn't exactly how things had gone but, by and large, Fazio had hit the mark.

'You can believe whatever you like. Did you find Spitaleri?'

'I tried him at home and his wife gave me his mobile number. At first there was no answer because it was turned off; then, an hour later, he picked up. He'll be here at nine sharp.'

'Find anything out?'

'Of course, Chief.' He pulled a little piece of paper out of his pocket and started to read. 'Michele Spitaleri, son of Bartolomeo Spitaleri and Maria Finocchiaro, born in Vigàta on the sixth of November 1960, currently residing in said city on via Lincoln 44, married to—'

'That's enough,' said Montalbano. 'I let you get some of it out of your system because I'm being nice today.'

'Thanks for that,' said Fazio.

'Tell me who this Spitaleri is.'

'Well, seeing as his sister married Pasquale Alessandro, and seeing as Alessandro has been Mayor of Vigàta for the last eight years, this Spitaleri happens to be the mayor's brother-in-law.'

'Elementary, my dear Watson.'

'Having, in that capacity, three construction companies and being a surveyor by trade, he gets ninety per cent of the municipality's contracts.'

'And they let him do that?'

'Yes, they do, because he pays his dues in equal part to the Cuffaros and the Sinagras. And, naturally, he kicks back a cut to his brother-in-law.'

And, therefore, since the Cuffaros and the Sinagras were the two dominant Mafia families in the area, the developer could consider himself safe.

'So the final cost of every contract ends up as double the amount established at the outset.'

'Dear Inspector, poor Spitaleri can't do it any differently or he'd be operating at a loss.'

'Anything else?'

Fazio looked vague. 'Rumours.'

'Meaning?'

'He really likes youngsters.'

'A paedophile?'

'Chief, I don't know what you'd call it, but the fact is, he likes young girls of around fourteen or fifteen.'

'But not sixteen?'

'No, he thinks they're past their prime.'

'He must be one of those who goes abroad, a "sex tourist".'

'Yessir, but he finds 'em here too. And he's not short of money. In town they say that once when a girl's mother and father wanted to report him, he paid out millions of lire and dodged the bullet. Another time, when he deflowered a virgin, he paid for it with an apartment.'

'And does he find people willing to sell him their daughters?'

'Chief, don't we live in a free-market economy, these days? And isn't the free market the sign of democracy, liberty and progress?'

Montalbano gawped at him, open-mouthed.

'Why are you looking at me like that?'

'Because you just said something I should have said . . .'

The telephone rang.

'Chief, there's a Mr Spitaleri here, says he gots—'

'Yes, send him in.' He turned to Fazio. 'Did you tell him why he was summoned?'

'Are you joking? Of course not.'

Spitaleri, tanned brown, dressed in a green jacket as light as onion skin and sporting a Rolex, shoulder-length hair, a gold bracelet, a gold crucifix that one could barely see amid the chest hair sticking out of his unbuttoned shirt, yellow moccasin loafers and no socks, was visibly nervous about being called in. The way he sat on the edge of the chair said it all. He spoke first. 'I came as you asked but, believe me, I have no idea—'

'You will.'

Why did the guy provoke such a violent aversion in him? Montalbano decided to put on the usual act to waste time.

'Fazio, have you finished over there with Franceschini?'

There was no Franceschini over there, but Fazio had a lot of experience playing the straight man. 'Not yet, sir.'

'I'll be right with you. Then we can finish this business in five minutes.'

Turning to Spitaleri, he stood up. 'Just sit tight a minute and then I'm all yours.'

'Look, Inspector, I have an engagement that—'

'I understand.'

They went into Fazio's office.

'Ask Catarella to make me some coffee in my pot. Would you like some?'

'No thanks, Chief.'

He took his time sipping his coffee, then went out to the car park to smoke a cigarette. Spitaleri had come in a black Ferrari. Which increased the inspector's dislike for the developer. Having a Ferrari in a small town was like keeping a lion in your apartment's bathroom.

When he returned to his office with Fazio, they found Spitaleri with his mobile phone to his ear, talking. '. . . to Filiberto. Listen, I'll get back to you later,' said Spitaleri, seeing them enter. He put his phone into his pocket.

'I see you were calling from here,' Montalbano said severely, beginning an improvisation worthy of the *commedia dell'arte*.

'Why? Am I not allowed to?' Spitaleri asked belligerently.

'You should have asked me.'

Spitaleri turned red with rage. 'I don't have to tell you anything! Until proven to the contrary, I'm a free citizen! If you have something to—'

'Calm down, Mr Spitaleri. You're making a mistake.'

'There's no mistake! You're treating me like someone under arrest!'

'Under arrest? Who said anything about arrest?'

'I want my lawyer!'

'Mr Spitaleri, please listen to what I have to tell you. Then you can decide whether or not to call your lawyer.'

'All right. Speak.'

'Now, then, if you had told me you wanted to phone someone, I would dutifully have informed you that all calls into and out of every police station in Italy, even those made with mobiles, are intercepted and recorded.'

'What?'

'Oh, yes. You heard correctly. A recent directive from the Ministry of the Interior. You know, with all the terrorism . . .'

Spitaleri had turned pale as a corpse. 'I want that tape!'

'You're always wanting something! Your lawyer, the tape . . .'

Fazio, the foil, started to laugh. 'Ha-ha-ha! He wants the tape!'

'Yes, I do. And I don't see what's funny about that!'

'Let me explain,' Montalbano interjected. 'We don't have any tapes here. The conversations are intercepted by the anti-Mafia and anti-terrorism commissions in Rome via satellite. And they are recorded there. To avoid all interference, deletion, omissions. Understand?'

Spitaleri was sweating so profusely he looked like a hot spring. 'Then what happens?'

'If, when they listen to the intercepted conversation, they hear anything suspicious, they inform us from Rome, and we investigate. Excuse me, but why are you so worried? You have no record, you're not a terrorist, you're not in the Mafia . . .'

'Of course, but . . .'

'But?'

'You see . . . about three weeks ago, at one of my work sites in Montelusa, there was an accident.'

Montalbano glanced at Fazio, who signalled to him that he knew nothing about it. 'What sort of accident?'

'A worker . . . an Arab . . .'

'An illegal immigrant?'

'Apparently, yes . . . But I had been assured . . .'

'. . . that he was legal.'

'Yes. Because he was in the process . . .'

'. . . of being legalized.'

'So you know everything!'

'Precisely.'

SIX

And, flashing a sly smile, he added, 'We know all about that case.'

'We certainly do!' Fazio laid it on even thicker, again laughing abrasively.

The lie was as big as a house.

'He fell from the scaffolding...' the inspector ventured.

'... on the third floor,' said Spitaleri, now drenched in sweat. 'It happened, as you probably know, on a Saturday. When there was no sign of him at the end of the day, everybody thought he'd already left. We didn't find out until Monday, when work resumed at the site.'

'Yeah, I know, that's what we were told by...'

'... Inspector Lozupone of Montelusa, who conducted a very serious investigation,' Spitaleri concluded.

'Right, Lozupone. By the way, what was the Arab's name again? I can't quite remember.'

'I can't remember, either.'

Montalbano thought they ought to build a great monument, like the Vittoriano in Rome to the Unknown Soldier, to commemorate all the illegal immigrants who had died on the job for a crust of bread.

'Well, you know, that business about the protective railing...'

A second shot in the dark.

'Oh, there was a protective railing, Inspector, I swear to God there was! Your colleague saw it with his own eyes. The truth of the matter is that that Arab was totally drunk, climbed over the railing and fell.'

'Are you aware of the post-mortem results?'

'Me? No.'

'No trace of alcohol was found in the blood.'

Another whopper. Montalbano was firing blindly away.

'But on his clothing there was!' said Fazio, with the usual laugh. He, too, was shooting blindly, come what may.

Spitaleri said nothing. He didn't even feign surprise.

'Who were you talking to just now?' the inspector asked, going back to square one.

'The yard foreman.'

'And what did you say to him? You don't have to answer, of course, but it's in your own best interests...'

'First, I told him I was sure you'd summoned me here to ask me about this business of the Arab and then—'

'That's enough, Signor Spitaleri, say no more,' said the inspector magnanimously. 'I am required to respect your privacy, you know. And I do so not out of formal observance of the law but out of a deep respect for others, which is something I was born with. If Rome tells me anything, I'll call you back here for questioning.'

Behind the developer's back, Fazio mimed clapping; he was applauding Montalbano's performance.

'So, I can go?'

'No.'

'Why not?'

'Well, you see, I didn't summon you here concerning the investigation into your employee's death, but about something else entirely. Do you remember if it was you who designed and built a house in the Pizzo district at Marina di Montereale?'

'For Angelo Speciale? Yes.'

'It is my duty to inform you that a crime was committed. We discovered some illegal construction, an entire underground level.'

Spitaleri could not hide his sigh of relief. Then he started to laugh. Had he expected a more serious charge? 'So, you found it! Well, you were wasting your time. That's pure nonsense, if you'll forgive me. Look, Inspector, around here you're practically required to engage in illegal construction just to avoid looking like an idiot! Everybody does it! All Speciale has to do is request an amnesty and—'

'That doesn't change the fact that you, as builder and works superintendent, didn't abide by the terms of the building permit.'

'But, Inspector, I repeat, that's bullshit!'

'It's a crime.'

'A crime, you say? I'd call it a minor error, the kind that used to be marked in red pencil. Believe me, you'd do better not to report me.'

'Are you threatening me, by any chance?'

'I'd never do that in the presence of a witness. It's just that, if you report me, you'll be the laughing stock of the town. You'll look like a fool.'

The fucking crook was getting bold. With that business about the phone call, he'd been practically shitting his pants, but illegal construction only made him laugh. So Montalbano decided to shoot him straight in the face. 'Maybe you're right. Unfortunately, however, I still have to look into that illegal apartment.'

'But why?'

'Because we found a dead body inside it.'

'A dead ... body?'

'Yes, of a fifteen-year-old girl. Little more than a child. With her throat slashed. A horror.'

He purposely stressed the words that referred to the victim's tender age.

Suddenly Spitaleri extended his arms, as if he was trying to fend off a force that was pushing him backwards. Then he attempted to stand up, but his legs and breath failed him and he fell back into the chair. 'Water!' he managed, with difficulty, to articulate.

*

They gave him the water, and even sent someone to fetch him a cognac from the bar on the corner.

'Feeling better?'

Spitaleri, who still didn't seem in any condition to speak, gestured with his hand that he felt so-so.

'Listen, Mr Spitaleri, for now I'll do the talking, and you can shake or nod your head. All right?'

The developer nodded.

'The girl's murder can only have happened on the day before or the day itself when the illegal apartment was buried. If it happened the day before, then the killer hid the body somewhere and only brought it inside the next day — and just in the nick of time, since the underground floor became inaccessible after that point. You follow?'

A nod.

'If, on the other hand, the murder took place on the day itself, the killer must have left just an opening, pushed the girl through it and then, once he was inside, raped her, slit her throat and stuck her into the trunk. After which he left the apartment and closed the only remaining opening. Do you agree?'

Spitaleri threw up his hands, as if to say he didn't know what to say.

'Did you oversee the work up to the last day?'

The developer shook his head. No.

'Why not?'

Spitaleri spread his arms and made a rumbling sound. 'Rrrrrrrrrrrrrh . . .'

Was he imitating an aeroplane?

'You were flying?'

Affirmative nod.

'How many masons were employed to bury the illegal apartment?'

Spitaleri held up two fingers.

Was this any way to carry on an investigation? It resembled a comedy routine.

'Mr Spitaleri, I'm tired of watching you answer in that fashion. Among other things, I'm beginning to wonder if you think we're so stupid that you can fuck around with us.' He turned to Fazio. 'Were you wondering the same thing?'

'I was.'

'So, you know what you're going to do? You're going to take him into the cloakroom, make him strip naked, then give him a cold shower until he recovers his senses.'

'I want my lawyer!' yelled Spitaleri, miraculously recovering his voice.

'You think it's a good idea to publicize this?'

'What do you mean?'

'I mean that if you call your lawyer I'll call the newsmen. I believe I remember you have a history with young girls ... If those guys turn it into a public trial, you're fucked. If, on the other hand, you cooperate, you can walk out of here in five minutes.'

Pale as a corpse, the developer was overcome by a

sudden fit of the shakes. 'What else do you want to know?'

'Just now you said you hadn't been able to see the work through to the end because you'd taken a plane somewhere. How many days before?'

'I left on the morning of the last day of work.'

'And do you remember when that last day was?'

'The twelfth of October.'

Fazio and Montalbano exchanged a glance.

'So, you're in a position to tell me whether, in the living room, aside from the window frames wrapped in plastic, there was also a trunk.'

'There was.'

'Are you sure about that?'

'Absolutely. And it was empty. Mr Speciale himself told us to carry it down there. He'd brought some stuff in it from Germany. It was rather battered and almost unusable, but he wanted it in the living room downstairs rather than throwing it away. He said he might need it later on.'

'Tell me the names of the two masons who were the last to work on the house.'

'I can't remember them.'

'Then you'd better phone your lawyer,' said Montalbano, 'because I'm going to accuse you of being an accessory to—'

'But I really can't remember!'

'I'm sorry, but—'

'Can I make a call to Dipasquale?'

'Who's he?'

'A foreman.'

'The one you called earlier?'

'Yes. That's him, Dipasquale. He was the foreman when we built Speciale's house.'

'Go ahead, but remember not to say anything that might compromise you. Don't forget the phone taps.'

Spitaleri dug out his mobile and dialled a number. 'Hello, 'Ngilino? 'S me. Do you by any chance remember the names of the masons who worked for us six years ago on the construction of the house at Pizzo, in Marina di Montereale? ... No? So what am I supposed to do? It's Inspector Montalbano who wants to know ... Oh, yes, that's true, you're right. Sorry.'

'Before I forget, would you give me Angelo Dipasquale's mobile-phone number? Fazio, write it down,' Montalbano directed him.

Spitaleri dictated it.

'So?' Montalbano pressed.

'Dipasquale can't remember the names of the masons, but they're definitely in my office somewhere. Can I go and get them?'

'Of course.'

The developer stood up and nearly ran to the door.

'Wait a minute. Fazio will go with you and will bring the names and addresses back to me. You, meanwhile, must remain available.'

'What does that mean?'

'It means you're not to leave the Vigàta area. If you need to go anywhere further away, you must let me know. Speaking of which, do you remember where you were flying to on the twelfth of October?'

'I ... To Bangkok.'

'You really like fresh meat, eh?'

*

The moment Spitaleri and Fazio had gone out, Montalbano phoned Spitaleri's foreman. He didn't want the developer to have time to talk to him and get their stories straight.

'Dipasquale? Inspector Montalbano here. How long would it take you to come down to the Vigàta police station from your work site?'

'Half an hour at most. But it's no use asking me 'cause I can't come now. I'm working.'

'I'm working, too. And my work involves telling you to come here now.'

'I repeat, I can't.'

'How would it be if I sent somebody to fetch you in one of our cars, sirens blaring, in front of all your men?'

'But what do you want?'

'Just come in and I'll satisfy your curiosity. You've got twenty-five minutes.'

*

He was there within twenty-two. To save time, he hadn't even changed his clothes. He was still in his lime-stained overalls. Dipasquale was about fifty; his hair was entirely white but he had a black moustache. Short and stocky, he never looked at the person he was speaking to, and when he did, his gaze was troubled.

'I don't understand why first you rang Mr Spitaleri about that Arab and then me about the house at Pizzo.'

'I didn't phone you about the house at Pizzo.'

'Oh? Why did you call me, then?'

'About the death of that Arab mason. What was his name?'

'I don't remember. But it was an accident! The guy was drunk! Those people start drinking first thing in the morning every day! Never mind Saturday! In fact, Inspector Lupuzone concluded that—'

'Forget my colleague's conclusions. Tell me exactly what happened.'

'But I've already told the judge and the inspector.'

'Third time lucky.'

'Oh, all right. At five thirty that Saturday, we finished working and left. Then, on Monday morning—'

'Stop. Didn't you notice that the Arab wasn't there?'

'No. What am I supposed to do – take a roll-call?'

'Who closes the work site?'

'The watchman, Filiberto – Filiberto Attanasio.'

But when they had come in and caught Spitaleri talking on the phone, hadn't he said that very name,

Filiberto? 'Why do you need a watchman? Don't you pay for protection?'

'There's always some young drug addict who might—'

'I see. Where can I find him?'

'Filiberto? He's the watchman at the site we're working at now. In fact, he sleeps there.'

'In the open air?'

'No, there's a hut made of corrugated tin.'

'Tell me the exact location of the construction site.'

Dipasquale told him.

'Go on.'

'But I've told you everything I know! We found the Arab dead on the Monday morning. He fell from the scaffolding on the third floor. He'd climbed over the protective railing, drunk as a skunk. It was an accident, I tell you!'

'For now, we'll stop there.'

'So I can go?'

'In just a minute. Were you there when the work was completed?'

Dipasquale baulked. 'But the construction in Montelusa's still not finished!'

'I'm talking about the house at Pizzo.'

'But didn't you say you called me in to talk about the Arab?'

'I've just changed my mind. Is that all right with you?'

'Have I any choice?'

'You know, of course, that a whole floor was built illegally at Pizzo?'

Dipasquale looked neither surprised nor concerned. 'Of course I know. But I was just following orders.'

'Do you know what the word "accomplice" means?'

'Yes.'

'Then tell me.'

'Well, there's accomplice and accomplice. To call somebody helping to build an illegal floor on a house an accomplice is like calling a pinprick a fatal injury.'

He even knew how to debate, did the foreman. 'Did you stay at Pizzo until the work was completed?'

'No. Mr Spitaleri transferred me to Fela four days before 'cause they were just finishing setting up another construction site there. But everything was just about done at Pizzo. We only had to seal off the illegal floor and cover it with sand. That was easy work, no need for a supervisor. I remember I hired two masons, but I forget their names. Like I said to Spitaleri, you can find them by looking—'

'Yes, Spitaleri went to turn them up. Listen, do you know if Mr Speciale stayed until the work was finished?'

'He was there as long as I was. And that mad stepson of his, the German kid.'

'Why did you call him mad?'

'Because he was.'

'What did he do that was so unusual?'

'He could stand on 'is head for an hour straight with

his feet in the air. An' he used to get down on all fours and eat grass like a sheep.'

'Is that all?'

'When nature called, he'd drop his trousers and do it in front of everybody without feeling embarrassed.'

'But nowadays there are a lot of people like him, no? They call themselves naturists, with good reason, I should think ... All things considered, it doesn't seem to me that this German was mad.'

'Wait. One day he went down to the beach. It was summertime and there was people there, and he got it in his head to strip bare-naked and start chasing a girl with 'is dick hanging out and all.'

'So what happened?'

'It turned out a couple of young guys who was there grabbed him and busted his head.'

Maybe Ralf had got it into his head to pretend he was Mallarmé's faun. But what the foreman was saying was interesting. 'Do you know of any other episodes like this one?'

'Yes. They told me he did the same thing with another young girl he met on that path that leads from the provincial road to Pizzo.'

'What did he do?'

'Soon as he saw her, he took off all his clothes and chased her.'

'And how did the girl get away?'

'Well, just then Mr Spitaleri drove by in his car.'

The right man at the right moment! A whole slew of clichés came into Montalbano's head: from the frying-pan into the fire, between a rock and a hard place ... He felt irked at himself for having such obvious thoughts. 'Listen, I suppose Mr Speciale knew about his stepson's exploits?'

'Oh, yes!'

'And what did he say about it?'

'Nothing. He just laughed. He said the boy had had his moments in Germany too, but was harmless. All he wanted to do to the girls was kiss 'em, that's what Mr Speciale told us. But what I want to know is this: why did he need to take off his clothes if all he wanted to do was kiss the girls?'

'All right, you can go now. But make yourself available to us.'

Dipasquale had spontaneously offered him Ralf's head on a platter not of silver but gold. Especially since the foreman, thus far, knew nothing about the murdered girl he'd found. So Montalbano had an embarrassment of riches to choose from, as far as sex maniacs went: Spitaleri and Ralf. There were just two minor problems. The young German had disappeared on his way back to Germany, and on that terrible 12 October, Spitaleri had been travelling.

SEVEN

Just to kill some time while he was waiting for Fazio to return, he decided to phone Forensics. 'I'd like to speak to Dr Arquà. Montalbano here.'

'Please hold.'

He had enough time to review the multiplication tables of six, seven, eight and nine in leisurely fashion.

'Inspector Montalbano? I'm sorry, but Dr Arquà is engaged at the moment.'

'And when will he be disengaged?'

'Please call back in about ten minutes.'

Engaged? Yes, to be married to his dog. The fucking idiot was playing hard to get. Getting precious. But how precious could an idiot get? And can an idiot increase in value?

*

He got up, left the room and, when passing Catarella, said, 'I'm going for a coffee at the port. I'll be back soon.'

Once outside, he realized he couldn't. In the car park the heat was similar to what one feels when standing in front of a blazing hearth. He touched the handle on the car door and burned himself. Cursing the saints, he went back inside. Catarella looked bewildered and glanced at his watch. He couldn't imagine how the inspector had managed to go to the port, drink a cup of coffee and get back in such a short time. 'Catarella, go and make me some coffee.'

'Anutter one, Chief? Din't you jes' have one? 'S not good to drink too much coffee.'

'You're right. Forget it.'

*

'I'd like to speak to Dr Arquà, if he's disengaged, that is. Montalbano here, same as before.'

'Please hold.'

No multiplication tables this time, but a few laborious attempts to sing a tune that must have been by the Rolling Stones, then another that was probably by the Beatles but came out almost the same as the first because he didn't quite have perfect pitch.

'Inspector Montalbano? Dr Arquà is still engaged. Try calling back –'

'– in about ten minutes, I know, I know.'

*

But why was he wasting all this time on an imbecile who was surely enjoying making him wait? He rolled two sheets of paper into a ball and stuck this into his mouth. Then he pinched his nostrils shut with a binder clip and redialled the forensic lab's number. He spoke with a slight Tuscan accent.

'This is Plenipotentiary Minister and Supervisor General Gianfilippo Maradona. Please connect me with Dr Arquà at once.'

'Straight away, Your Excellency.'

Montalbano spat out the ball of paper and removed the clamp.

Half a minute later, Arquà came on the line. 'Good day, Your Excellency, what can I do for you?'

'Why are you calling me "Your Excellency?" This is Montalbano.'

'But I was told—'

'But you can keep calling me that, I rather like it.'

Arquà let a few moments of silence pass. It was clear that he was tempted to hang up, but then he made up his mind. 'What do you want?'

'Do you have anything to tell me?'

'Yes.'

'Then tell me.'

'You're supposed to say "please".'

'Please.'

'Question.'

'Where was she killed?'

'Where she was found.'

'In exactly the same place?'

'Next to what would have been the french windows in the living room.'

'Are you sure about that?'

'Absolutely.'

'Why?'

'Because a pool of blood had even formed there.'

'Anywhere else?'

'No, nothing.'

'Just that pool?'

'There were streaks from her having been dragged from the pool to a spot next to the trunk.'

'Did you find the weapon?'

'No.'

'Fingerprints?'

'A billion.'

'Even on the plastic wrapped round the body?'

'Nothing there.'

'Did you find anything else?'

'The roll of packing tape. The same that was used for the window frames.'

'No fingerprints there either?'

'Nothing.'

'Is that all?'

'That's all.'

'Fuck you.'

'Same to you.'

Nice exchange. Terse and crisp as a dialogue from one of Vittorio Alfieri's tragedies.

One thing, however, had come out of it: that the killing had to have taken place on the masons' last day of work.

*

He couldn't stay in his office any longer. His brain felt reduced to a kind of dense jam in which his thoughts had trouble circulating and sometimes got stuck.

Was a chief inspector allowed to go bare-chested in his office? Was there a rule prohibiting this? No. One needed only to hope that no outsider came in unannounced.

He got up and closed the shutter to the window, through which no air was passing, only heat. He half shut the inside blinds, turned on the light, and removed his shirt. 'Catarella!'

'Coming!'

When Catarella saw him, he said, 'Lucky youse that can do it!'

'Listen, don't let anyone in without telling me first. I mean it. And another thing. Call a shop that sells fans and have a rather big one delivered here.'

*

Since there was still no sign of Fazio, he dialled another number. 'Dr Pasquano? Montalbano here.'

'Would you believe it? I was actually just now regretting that no one was on my back.'

'See? I sensed it and took immediate action.'

'What the fuck do you want?'

The usual refined, aristocratic courtesy from Pasquano. 'Don't you know?'

'I'm going to work on that girl this afternoon. Ring me tomorrow morning.'

'Not tonight?'

'Tonight I'm going to the club. I've got a serious poker game to attend, and I don't want any—'

'I understand. So, you didn't give the body even a superficial glance?'

'Very superficial.'

From the way he had said it, the inspector gathered that the doctor had arrived at some sort of conclusion. The problem was handling him the right way.

'You're going to the club around nine, right?'

'Yes. Why?'

'Because around ten I'm going to turn up at the club with a couple of uniformed men and raise such a stink that I'll fuck up your poker game.' Montalbano heard him chuckle. 'So, what do you say?'

'I can confirm that she wasn't more than sixteen.'

'And?'

'The killer slit her throat.'

'With what?'

'With one of those knives you carry around in your

pocket, but which are sharp as razors. Like the Opinel brand.'

'Could you tell if he was left-handed?'

'Yes, if I look into a crystal ball.'

'Is that so hard to establish?'

'Hard enough. And I don't feel like bullshitting.'

'I do it all the time! Let me have the satisfaction of hearing you bullshit just once.'

'Look, it's just a hypothesis, mind, but in my opinion the murderer was not left-handed.'

'On what do you base that statement?'

'I got a certain sense of the position.'

'What position?'

'Haven't you ever happened to leaf through the *Kama Sutra*?'

'Explain what you mean.'

'Look, let me repeat my disclaimer that this is just a theory. The man persuades the girl to follow him into the part of the house that is now almost entirely covered with sandy soil. Once he's got her inside, he has only two thoughts in his head. The first is to fuck her, the second is to find the right moment for killing her.'

'So, you think it was premeditated murder, not temporary insanity or something similar?'

'I'm merely explaining my own conjecture.'

'But why did he want to kill her?'

'Maybe they'd already had sex, and the girl had asked him for a lot of money to keep quiet. You have to bear in mind that she was a minor, and it's quite possible the man was married. Don't you think that's a good motive?'

'Yes, in fact.'

'Can I go on?'

'Of course.'

'The man tells her to take all her clothes off, which he does, too, and then to bend down in front of him, bracing herself with her hands against the wall, as he fucks her from behind. When the time is right—'

'Will the post-mortem be able to establish if she had had sex?'

'Six years later? Are you mad? Anyway, I was saying, when the time is right—'

'What's that supposed to mean?'

'As the girl is reaching orgasm and is therefore not in a position to react promptly.'

'Go on.'

'– he grabs the knife.'

'Stop. Where does he grab it from, if he's naked?'

'How the fuck should I know where he gets it from? Look, if you keep interrupting me, I'm going to change the story and tell you *Snow White and the Seven Dwarfs* instead.'

'Sorry. Please continue.'

'He grabs the knife – you can figure out yourself where from – cuts her throat and, shoving her forward, he jumps backwards. He waits for her to bleed to death, then spreads a big sheet of plastic across the floor. After all, there are so many lying about—'

'Wait a second. Before grabbing the sheet of plastic, he puts on latex gloves.'

'Why?'

'Because there are no fingerprints on that plastic. Arquà told me. Or on the adhesive tape.'

'You see? It was all premeditated. He even had the gloves in his pocket! Shall I go on?'

'Yes.'

'He wraps up the body and puts it into the trunk. When he's finished, he gets dressed. He probably hasn't got a single drop of blood on his skin.'

'What about the girl's clothes, underwear and shoes?'

'Nowadays girls go around very lightly dressed. All the man would have needed was a plastic bag to make off with them.'

'Okay, but why did he make off with them instead of putting them inside the trunk?'

'I don't know. It could have been an irrational move. Murderers don't always behave rationally. You know that better than I do. Is that enough for you?'

'Yes and no.'

'Or else he might be a fetishist who, every now and then, pulls out the girl's clothes, sniffs them to smell her scent and wanks to his heart's content.'

'But how did you arrive at this conclusion?'

'About the wanking, you mean?'

Pasquano was in a playful mood. 'I was referring to your reconstruction of the murder.'

'Oh, that. By looking closely at how and where the tip of the knife went in, and by considering the line of the cut. Among other things, the girl kept her head down, with her chin touching her chest, and this helped me work out the way things went, given that the murderer also slashed her right cheek as he was pulling the knife out of her throat.'

'Any distinguishing marks?'

'For identification? She had an appendectomy scar and a rare congenital malformation on her right foot.'

'Namely?'

'Varus in the big toe.'

'In plain words?'

'It was bent inwards.'

✢

All of a sudden he remembered something he should have done at once but had forgotten. It was certainly not old age that had made him forget it, he reassured himself, but the heat, which had the same effect as three sleeping pills.

'Catarella? Come into my office.'

A quarter of a second later he materialized. 'Your orders, sir.'

'I need you to do a search on the computer.'

''Ass what I'm here for, Chief.'

'Find out if anyone ever reported the disappearance of a sixteen-year-old girl around the thirteenth or fourteenth of October 1999.'

'I'll get on it straight aways.'

'And what about that fan?'

'Chief, I called four differin shops. The fans're all sold out. One guy told me all he had was balls.'

'What kind of balls?'

'The kind you attach to the ceiling. I'll try a few more.'

*

The inspector waited half an hour, and since there was still no sign of Fazio, he went out to eat. Merely getting into his car and driving the short stretch of road to the trattoria was enough to drench his shirt.

'Inspector,' said Enzo, 'it's too hot for hot food.'

'So what have you got?'

'How about a few big platters of *antipasto di mare* with shrimps, prawns, baby octopus, anchovies, sardines, mussels and clams?'

'Sounds good. And for the second course?'

'Mullet in onions: served cold, a delight. Then, at the end, to cleanse the palate, my wife made some lemon sorbet.'

*

ANDREA CAMILLERI

Either because of the heat or because of his stomach, which felt very heavy, he skipped his customary walk along the jetty and went straight home.

Opening all the windows and doors in the vain hope of creating even the slightest draught, he lay down naked on the bed, on top of the sheets, for an hour's nap. Then, when he awoke, he put on his swimming trunks and went for a swim, risking heart failure.

*

He had cooled himself off nicely and, once back in the house, felt like hearing Livia's voice. What to do? He decided to set aside his pride and telephone her.

'Oh, it's you,' said Livia, sounding neither surprised nor glad. Actually, let's admit it: she was downright Antarctic.

'How was the drive back?'

'Horrendous. Hot as hell. The car's air-conditioning broke. Then, when we stopped at an Autogrill after Grosseto, Bruno disappeared.'

'That child has a gift for it.'

'Please, don't start.'

'I was merely stating a fact. Where did he end up?'

'We lost two hours looking for him. He'd hidden inside a tractor cab.'

'What about the driver?'

'He hadn't noticed. He was asleep. Now, I have to go.'

'Where to?'

'My cousin Massimiliano is waiting for me downstairs. You caught me purely by chance – I'd come up to get some clothes.'

'Where have you been?'

'With Guido and Laura, at their villa.'

'And now you're leaving?'

'Yes, with Massimiliano. We're going on a little cruise in his boat.'

'How many of you are there?'

'Just him and me. 'Bye.'

''Bye.'

And where the hell did her dear cousin Massimiliano find the money to maintain a cruiser, considering that he didn't work and spent his days counting flies? Montalbano would have done better not to have made the call.

He was about to leave the house when the telephone rang.

'Hello?'

'Most of all, you're a man who doesn't keep his word!'

It was Livia, apparently spoiling for a fight.

'Me?'

'Yes, you!'

'Would you mind telling me when I didn't keep my word?'

'You swore to me that there were no murders in Vigàta during the summer.'

'How can you make such a statement? I swore? At the most, I probably said that, with the summer heat, the people planning to kill someone decide to postpone it till autumn.'

'So how is it that Guido and Laura ended up sharing their bed with a murder victim in the middle of August?'

'Livia, stop exaggerating! Sharing their bed!'

'Well, practically.'

'Listen carefully. That murder dates from the month of October six years ago. October, did you get that? Which means, among other things, that my theory was not just hot air.'

'What matters to me is that all because of you—'

'All because of me? If that little imp Bruno hadn't given in to the temptation to emulate Houdini—'

'Houdi-who?'

'Houdini, a famous magician. If Bruno hadn't gone and disappeared underground, nobody would have known there was a corpse downstairs, and your friends could have gone on sleeping soundly.'

'Your cynicism is repugnant.' She hung up.

*

When he got back to the station, it was almost six o'clock.

He had wanted to go in earlier, but when he stepped outside his house, he was assailed by a blast of heat so intense that he went back in. Taking his clothes off, he filled the tub with cold water and lay in it for an hour.

*

'Aaah Chief, Chief! I found 'er. I idinnificated the girl!'
Arms extended away from his body, fingers stretched and
spread out, he was strutting like a peacock.

'Come into my office.'

Catarella followed him with a sheet of paper in hand
and an attitude so exultant that one could almost hear, in
the background, the triumphal march of *Aida*.

EIGHT

Montalbano glanced at the file that Catarella had printed out for him.

> MORREALE, Caterina, known as 'Rina'
> daughter of Giuseppe Morreale and Francesca Dibetta
> born in Vigàta on 7 March 1983
> residing in Vigàta, at via Roma 42
> disappeared 12 October 1999
> reported missing by father on 13 October 1999
> Height: 5 ft. 9 in.
> Hair: blonde
> Eyes: blue
> Build: slender
> Distinguishing marks: small scar from appendectomy and
>   varus of right big toe
>
> NOTE: Bulletin issued by Fiacca Central Police

*

He pushed away the sheet of paper, buried his face in his hands. Throat slashed worse than if she'd been a sheep, or any kind of animal at all. Now that he'd seen, from the accompanying photo, what she had looked like, he felt sure, for no apparent reason, that Dr Pasquano was simultaneously right and wrong.

He was right when he told him how she'd been killed, but wrong about why she'd been killed. Pasquano had advanced the hypothesis of blackmail, but Rina Morreale, with her serene blue eyes, would never have been capable of blackmail.

Even if she had consented to making love with the man who would later kill her, how could she ever have followed him underground of her own accord, into an illegal apartment that one entered through a narrow, even dangerous opening? Above all, it must have been pitch-dark down there. Had the murderer perhaps brought a torch with him?

But hadn't there been a better place? Couldn't they have done it in a car? Pizzo was a secluded spot; it wouldn't have been a problem.

No, Rina Morreale was definitely forced by the killer to enter what was to become her tomb.

Catarella had come up beside him to look at the photograph of the girl. Maybe he hadn't paid much attention to it before.

'She was so beauty-full!' he said softly, moved.

The photo was consistent with the description and

showed a girl of rare beauty. Her neck looked as if it had been painted by Botticelli.

There was no need to do any more searches. He had only to inform the family so that somebody could go to Montelusa to identify the body. Montalbano's heart ached.

'She was so beauty-full!' Catarella repeated in a low voice.

Looking up, the inspector caught him turned three-quarters away, drying his eyes on the sleeve of his jacket.

Better change the subject at once. 'Is Fazio back?'

'Yessir.'

'Could you call him for me?'

Fazio, too, had a sheet of paper in his hand when he came in. 'Catarella told me the girl's been identified. Can I see her?'

Montalbano handed him the printout. Fazio looked at it, then gave it back to him. 'Poor kid.'

'When we catch him – because we will catch him, of that much I'm certain – I'm going to smash his face in,' the inspector said quietly. A thought had just come to him. 'How is it,' he continued, 'that the girl's parents reported her missing to the Fiacca police?'

'I don't understand it, Chief, even though it happened during the period of co-operation between all the different commissariats regardless of territorial boundaries. Remember all the confusion?'

'How could I not? Since we had to deal with everything, we couldn't deal with anything. Anyway, let's not forget to ask the parents.'

'Speaking of which, who's going to tell them?'

'You are. But inform Tommaseo first. In fact, do that now, from this phone. Then we won't have to think about it any more.'

Fazio spoke with the prosecutor, who wanted the file emailed to him. But before alerting the parents, the inspector wanted to talk to Pasquano and assure himself of the girl's identity.

'Catarella!'

'Here I am, Chief.'

'Take the girl's file and email it immediately to Prosecutor Tommaseo.'

After Catarella had gone. Montalbano went on the attack. 'Why did it take you all morning to find those names?'

'It wasn't my job to find them, Chief, it was Spitaleri's.'

'But haven't they got a computer or some other sort of filing system?'

'They have, but they keep only the information of the last five years in the office, and since that house was built six years ago . . .'

'And where do they keep the rest of it?'

'At the house of Spitaleri's sister, who, it turns out, went to Montelusa this morning so we had to wait till she got back.'

'I don't understand why he keeps these documents at his sister's house.'

'I do.'

'Then tell me.'

'Because of the Finance Police. In the event of an unannounced visit by the auditors. That way, Spitaleri has time to forewarn his sister. Who has been instructed beforehand and knows which documents to bring and which not to bring to the office. Does that explain it?' Fazio asked.

'Perfectly.'

'Anyway, the masons who were working—'

'Wait a minute. We still haven't had a chance to talk about Spitaleri.'

'Concerning the girl's murder—'

'No. For now I want to talk about Spitaleri the property developer. Not the Spitaleri who likes under-age girls. We can talk about him afterwards. What did you make of him?'

'Chief, he smells fishy to me. When we made up the story about the post-mortem not finding any alcohol in the Arab's blood but only on his clothes, he didn't react. Not a peep. He should have either been surprised or said it couldn't be true.'

'Therefore they must have drenched the poor bastard in wine after he died so people would think he'd been drunk.'

'So what do you think happened, Chief?'

'When you were out with Spitaleri, I called in the foreman, Dipasquale, and interrogated him. In my opinion, the Arab fell off the unprotected scaffolding and none of his comrades noticed. Maybe he was working alone in some concealed area of the structure. Then the site's watchman, whose name is Filiberto Attanasio, found the body after everybody'd gone home and rang Dipasquale, who informed Spitaleri. What's wrong? Are you listening to me?'

Fazio looked lost in thought. 'What did you say the watchman's name was?'

'Filiberto Attanasio.'

'Would you excuse me for a minute?' He got up, went out, and returned five minutes later with a printout in hand. 'I remember him well,' he said.

He handed Montalbano the printout. Filiberto Attanasio had been convicted several times of theft, grievous bodily harm, attempted murder and armed robbery. The photo showed a fiftyish man with an oversized nose and nary a hair on his head. He was classified as a habitual offender.

'A good thing to know,' was the inspector's comment. Then he said, 'After being informed by the watchman, they checked out the situation and decided to cover their arses by putting up a protective railing, which they didn't have, at the crack of dawn on Sunday. They drenched the body in wine and went home to bed. The following morning, thanks to the watchman, they sorted it all out.'

'And Inspector Lozupone swallowed it.'

'You think so? Do you know Lozupone?'

'Not personally. But I'm certainly aware of who he is.'

'I've known him a long time. He's not—'

The phone rang.

'Chief? 'At'd be Proxeter Dommaseo onna phone wanting a talk to you poissonally in poisson.'

'Put him on.'

'Montalbano? Tommaseo.'

'Tommaseo? Montalbano.'

The prosecutor got disoriented. 'I wanted to tell you … er … Ah, yes, I've seen the photo on the printout. What a beautiful girl.'

'Right.'

'Raped and slaughtered!'

'Did Dr Pasquano tell you she'd been raped?'

'No. He told me only that her throat had been slashed. But I sense intuitively that she was raped. In fact, I'm sure of it.'

As if the public prosecutor's brain wouldn't be working round the clock trying to imagine, down to the finest detail, the crime scene.

At this moment, Montalbano had a truly brilliant idea that might perhaps spare him or Fazio the unpleasant task of breaking the tragic news to the girl's family. 'Apparently the girl has a twin sister, or so I've been told, who is far more beautiful than the victim,' he said.

'More beautiful? Really?'

'Apparently, yes.'

'So, today this twin sister would be twenty-two years old.'

'It adds up.'

Fazio was glaring at him, dumbfounded. What on earth was the inspector concocting?

There was a pause. Surely the prosecutor, his eyes glued to the photo in the dossier, was licking his chops at the thought of meeting the twin sister. Then he spoke. 'Montalbano, I think it would be better if I went in person to inform the family ... given the victim's tender age ... and the particularly savage manner ...'

'You're absolutely right, sir. You're a man of profound human understanding. So you'll tell the family?'

'Yes. It seems only right.'

They said goodbye and hung up. Fazio, having understood the inspector's game, was laughing. 'The minute that man hears talk of a woman ...'

'Forget about him. He'll dash over to the Morreales' house, hoping to meet a twin sister who doesn't exist. What was I saying to you before he called?'

'You were telling me about Inspector Lozupone.'

'Ah, yes. Lozupone's been around, he's clever, and he knows what's what.'

'What's that supposed to mean?'

'That in all likelihood Lozupone thought as we did, that the protective railing was put up after the accident, but he let it slide.'

'And why would he do that?'

'Maybe he was advised to stick to what Dipasquale and Spitaleri were telling him. But it's unlikely we'll ever find out who, in the commissariat or in the Ministry of so-called Justice, gave him this advice.'

'Well, we might be able to get some idea, anyway,' said Fazio.

'How?'

'Chief, you said you know Lozupone well. But do you know who he's married to?'

'No.'

'Dr Lattes's daughter.'

'Ah.'

Not bad, as news went.

Dr Lattes, chief of the commissioner's cabinet, dubbed 'Caffe-Lattes' for his cloying manner, was a man of church and prayer, a man who never said a word without first anointing it with lubricant, and who was continuously, at the right and wrong moments, giving thanks to the Blessed Virgin Mary.

'Do you know what political formation Spitaleri's brother-in-law is with?'

'You mean the mayor? Mayor Alessandro is with the same party as the regional president, which happens to be the same party as Dr Lattes, and he's the grand delegate of the Honourable MP Catapano, which is saying a lot.'

Gerardo Catapano was a man who had managed to keep both the Cuffaros and the Sinagras, the two Mafia families of Vigàta, on good behaviour.

Montalbano felt momentarily demoralized. How could it be that things never changed? *Mutatis mutandis*, one always ended up caught in dangerous webs of relations, collusions between the Mafia and politicians, the Mafia and entrepreneurs, politicians and banks, money-launderers and loan sharks.

What an obscene ballet! What a petrified forest of corruption, fraud, rackets, villainy, business! He imagined a likely dialogue.

'Proceed very carefully because Z, who is MP Y's man and the son-in-law of K, who is Mafia boss Z's man, enjoys particularly good relations with MP H.'

'But doesn't MP H belong to the opposition party?'

'Yes, but it's the same thing.'

How had Papa Dante put it?

> Ah, servile Italy, you are sorrow's hostel,
> a ship without helmsman in terrible storms,
> lady not of the provinces, but of a brothel!

Italy was still servile, obeying at least two masters, America and the Church, and the storms had become a daily occurrence, thanks to a helmsman whom she would have been better off without. Of course, the provinces of which Italy was the 'lady' now numbered more than a hundred, but the brothel, for its part, had increased exponentially.

'So, about those six masons ...' Fazio resumed.

'Wait. Have you got things to do this evening?'

'No, sir.'

'Would you come with me to Montelusa?'

'What for?'

'To have a little chat with Filiberto, the watchman. I know how to find the site – Dipasquale explained it to me.'

'It seems to me, sir, that you want to harm this Spitaleri.'

'You've hit the nail on the head.'

'Of course I'll come along.'

'So, are you going to tell me about these masons or not?'

Fazio gave him a dirty look. 'Chief, I've been trying to tell you for the past hour.' He unfolded his sheet of paper. 'The masons' names are as follows: Antonio Dalli Cardillo, Ermete Smecca, Ignazio Butera, Antonio Passalacqua, Stefano Fiorillo, Gaspare Miccichè. Dalli Cardillo and Miccichè are the two who worked until the end and covered up the illegal ground floor.'

'If I ask you a question, will you answer me truthfully?'

'I'll try.'

'Did you dig up the complete vital statistics on each of these six masons?'

Fazio blushed slightly. He could not control his 'records-office mania', as the inspector called it. 'Yes, Chief, I did. But I didn't read them to you.'

'You didn't read them to me because you didn't have the courage. Did you find out if and where they work?'

'Of course. They're currently on the four construction sites Spitaleri's got going.'

'Four?'

'Yessir. And in five days another's opening. With the connections he's got between politicos and Mafiosi, how could he ever be short of work? Anyway, to conclude, Spitaleri told me he prefers always to use the same masons.'

'Except for the occasional Arab he can toss into the dustbin without too much fuss. Are Dalli Cardillo and Miccichè working at the Montelusa site?'

'No.'

'So much the better. I want you to call those two in for questioning tomorrow morning, one for ten o'clock and the other for noon, since we'll probably be up late tonight. And don't accept any excuses. Threaten them if you need to.'

'I'll get on to it straight away.'

'Good. I'm going home. We'll meet back here at midnight, and then we'll head for Montelusa.'

'Okay. Should I put on my uniform?'

'You must be kidding. Much better for the man to think we're somewhat shady.'

✷

Sitting on the veranda at Marinella, he thought he felt a hint of cool, but it was mostly a hypothesis of cool since neither the sea nor the air was moving.

Adelina had made *pappanozza* for him. Onions and potatoes boiled for a long time and mashed with the back of a fork until they blended together. For seasoning: olive oil, a hint of vinegar, salt and freshly ground black pepper. It was all he ate. He wanted to stick to light food.

Then he sat outside until eleven o'clock, reading a good detective novel by two Swedish authors, husband and wife, in which there wasn't a page without a ferocious and justified attack on social democracy and the government. In his mind Montalbano dedicated the book to all those who did not deign to read mystery novels because, in their opinion, they were only entertaining puzzles.

At eleven he turned on the television. *Lupus in fabula*: TeleVigàta featured a story showing the honourable Gerardo Catapano inaugurating the new municipal dog shelter of Montelusa.

He turned it off, freshened up a bit and left the house.

✷

He arrived at the station at a quarter to midnight. Fazio was already there. Both men were wearing a light jacket over a short-sleeved shirt. They smiled at one another for having had the same idea. Anyone wearing a jacket in that extreme heat couldn't help but cause alarm, since ninety-nine times out of a hundred it served to hide the revolver he was carrying in his waistband or pocket.

And, in fact, they were both armed.

'Shall we go in mine or yours?'

'Yours.'

It took them scarcely half an hour to drive to the site, which was near the old Montelusa railway station.

They parked and got out. The site was surrounded by wooden fencing almost six and a half feet high and had a big, locked gate.

'Do you remember,' said Fazio, 'what used to be here?'

'No.'

'Palazzina Linares.'

Montalbano remembered it. A little jewel from the second half of the nineteenth century that the Linares, rich sulphur merchants, had hired Giovan Battista Basile, the famous architect of the Teatro Massimo in Palermo, to build. Later the Linares had fallen into ruin, and so had their *palazzina*. Instead of restoring it, the authorities had decided to demolish it and build, in its place, an eight-storey block of flats. So strict, the Ministry of Culture!

They walked up to the wooden gate, peered between the fenceposts but saw no lights on.

Fazio pushed the gate softly three times. 'It's locked from the inside with a bolt.'

'Think you could climb over and open it?'

'Yes, but not here. A car might drive by. I'll get over the fence at the back. You wait for me here.'

'Be careful. There may be a dog.'

'I don't think so. It would have started barking by now.'

The inspector had time to smoke a cigarette before the gate opened just enough to let him in.

NINE

It was pitch-dark inside. To the right, however, one could make out a shed.

'I'll fetch the torch,' said Fazio.

When he returned, he re-bolted the gate and turned on the torch. As they cautiously approached the door to the shed, they noticed it was half open. Apparently, in this heat, Filiberto couldn't stand being inside with the door closed. Then they heard him snoring lustily.

'We mustn't give him any time to think,' Montalbano whispered into Fazio's ear. 'Don't turn on the lights. We'll work him over with the torch beam. We need to frighten him to death.'

'No problem,' said Fazio.

They entered on tiptoe. The shed stank of sweat, and the smell of wine was so strong that one felt drunk just breathing it. Filiberto, in his underpants, was lying on a camp-bed. He was the same man as in the dossier's photograph.

Fazio shone the torch round the room. The watchman's clothes hung from a nail. There was a little table, two chairs, a small enamel wash-basin on an iron tripod, and a jerry-can. Montalbano grabbed it and smelled it: water. Without making any noise, he filled the basin, then picked it up in both hands, approached the camp-bed and flung the water into Filiberto's face. The man opened his eyes and, blinded by Fazio's torch, closed them at once, then opened them again, raising a hand to shield himself. 'Who – who—'

'Whoopeedoo!' said Montalbano. 'Don't move.'

And he brought his pistol into the torch beam. Filiberto instinctively put up his hands.

'Have you got a mobile phone?' the inspector asked.

'Yes.'

'Where is it?'

'In my jacket.'

The one hanging from the nail. The inspector grabbed the phone, dropped it on to the floor and stamped on it.

Filiberto mustered the courage to ask, 'Who are you?'

'Friends, Filibè. Get up.'

Filiberto stood up.

'Turn round.'

His hands shaking slightly, Filiberto turned his back to them. 'But what do you want? Spitaleri's always paid his dues!'

'Shut up!' Montalbano ordered. 'Say your prayers.'

And he cocked the pistol.

Hearing that dry, metallic click, Filiberto's legs turned to pudding and he fell to his knees. 'For heaven's sake! I ain't done nothing! Why do you want to kill me?' he asked, weeping.

Fazio kicked his shoulder, making him fall forward. Montalbano put the barrel of the pistol to the nape of his neck. 'You listen to me,' he began. Then he stopped. 'He's either dead or fainted.' He bent down to touch the jugular on the man's neck. 'He fainted. Sit him up in a chair.'

Fazio handed Montalbano the torch, grabbed the watchman by the armpits and sat him down. But he had to hold him up because he kept sliding to one side. They both noticed that the man's underpants were wet. Filiberto had pissed himself in fear. Montalbano went up to him and dealt him such a slap that he opened his eyes. The watchman blinked repeatedly, disoriented, then immediately started crying again. 'Don't kill me, please!'

'You answer our questions, you save your life,' said Montalbano, holding the pistol to his face.

'I'll answer! I'll answer!'

'When the Arab fell, was there any protective railing?'

'What Arab?'

Montalbano put the barrel to his forehead. 'When the Arab mason fell . . .'

'Aah, yes, no, there wasn't.'

'Did you put it up on Sunday morning?'

'Yessir.'

'You, Spitaleri and Dipasquale?'

'Yessir.'

'Whose idea was it to douse the dead body with wine?'

'Spitaleri's.'

'Now, be careful. Make no mistakes when you answer. Did you already have the materials for the railing at the construction site?'

The question was essential to Montalbano. Everything hinged on Filiberto's answer.

'No, sir. Spitaleri ordered it an' it was brought here early on Sunday morning.'

It was the best answer the inspector could have hoped for. 'Who supplied it? What company?'

'Ribaudo's.'

'Did you sign the receipt?'

'Yessir.'

Montalbano congratulated himself. He'd not only hit the nail on the head, he had even found out what he'd wanted to know. Now they needed to add some drama to the drama, for the benefit of the boss, Spitaleri. 'Why didn't you get the stuff from Milluso's?'

'How should I know?'

'And to think we told Spitaleri a thousand times, "You've got to use Milluso's! You've got to use Milluso's!" But *noooo* ... He wants to play the smartarse with us. He doesn't want to understand. So now we're going to kill you so he finally gets it.'

With the strength of desperation, Filiberto leaped to

his feet. But he had no time to do anything else. From behind, Fazio clubbed him on the side of the neck.

The watchman fell and didn't move.

They raced outside, opened the gate, got into the car and, as Fazio was turning on the ignition, Montalbano said, 'See how, if you're nice, you can have anything you want?' Then he stopped talking.

*

As they were driving back to Vigàta, Fazio commented, 'That was just like an American movie!' And, since the inspector just sat there in silence, he asked, 'Are you counting up how many crimes we committed?'

'Let's not think about it.'

'Are you dissatisfied with the answers Filiberto gave you?'

'No, on the contrary.'

'So what's wrong?'

'I don't like what I did.'

'I'm sure the guy didn't recognize us.'

'Fazio, I didn't say we did anything wrong, I said I didn't like it.'

'You mean the way we treated Filiberto?'

'Yes.'

'But, Chief, he's a criminal!'

'And we're not?'

'If we hadn't done what we did, he wouldn't have talked.'

'That's not a good reason.'

'What do you want us to do? Go back and tell him we're sorry?' Fazio snapped.

Montalbano said nothing. A minute later, Fazio said, 'I apologize, sir.'

'Oh, come on!'

'Do you think Spitaleri will swallow the story that we were sent by Milluso's outfit?'

'It'll take him two or three days to work out that Milluso's had nothing to do with it. But those two or three days will be enough for me.'

'There's one thing I still don't understand,' said Fazio.

'Tell me.'

'Why, when he needed the material for the railing, did he turn to Ribaudo's instead of having it sent from one of his other sites?'

'That would have meant involving other people from these sites. Spitaleri must have thought that the fewer people who knew about it, the better. Apparently he could trust Ribaudo's.'

*

During the night Montalbano's consciousness, contrary to his fears, chose to rest. Thus he awoke from his five hours of sleep as if he had slept ten. The cloudless morning sky put him in a good mood. Even at that early hour, though, the air was hot.

The minute he arrived at the office, he phoned Marshal Alberto Laganà, of the Finance Police, who had helped him many times before.

'Inspector! What a pleasant surprise! What's the good news?'

'It's bad news, unfortunately.'

'Let's hear it anyway.'

'Do you know the Ribaudo firm in Vigàta, the one that supplies construction materials?'

Laganà chuckled to himself. 'You bet we know them! Materials sold without invoices, evasion of sales tax, cooking the books … And we were planning to renew our acquaintance in the next few days.'

A stroke of excellent luck. 'When, exactly?'

'Three days from now.'

'Couldn't you start early, say, tomorrow?'

'But tomorrow is the fifteenth of August! What's this about?'

Montalbano explained the situation to him. And told him what he wanted to know.

'I think I can manage it the day after tomorrow,' Laganà concluded.

*

'Chief? There's summon says he's called Falli Fardillo that says you summoned 'im for ten aclack this morning.'

'Have you got the printout on the girl who was killed?'

125

'Yessir.'

'Bring it to me, then tell Fazio to come to my office and lastly, send that man in.'

Naturally, Catarella sent in Dalli Cardillo first, then went and got the file, which Montalbano placed upside-down on his desk, and finally called Fazio.

Dalli Cardillo was thick-set and fiftyish, with short-cropped hair that lacked a trace of white. He was swarthy and sporting a moustache of the sort that Turks used to wear in the nineteenth century. He was nervous, and it showed.

But who isn't nervous when summoned without explanation to the police station? Wait a second. Without explanation? Was it possible Spitaleri hadn't already told him what to say? 'Signor Dalli Cardillo, did Mr Spitaleri tell you why you were summoned here?'

'No, sir.'

He seemed sincere to Montalbano. 'Do you remember working on one of Spitaleri's sites six years ago, when you built a house in the Pizzo district of Marina di Montereale?'

Hearing the question, the mason looked so relieved that he allowed himself a little smile. 'Did you discover the illegal floor?' he asked.

'Yes.'

'I did what the boss told me to do.'

'I'm not accusing you of anything. All I want from you is some information.'

'As far as that goes, I'm at your service.'

'Was it you, with your colleague Gaspare Miccichè, who covered the lower apartment with sandy soil?'

'Yessir.'

'Did you work together the whole time?'

'No. That day I finished at twelve thirty, and Miccichè continued alone.'

'Why did you stop early?'

'Mr Spitaleri's orders.'

'But hadn't he already left?'

'Yes, but the day before he went, he told us what to do.'

'Could you explain to me how you got in and out of the bottom floor?'

'We made a sort of tunnel out of wooden planks, a kind of covered, sloping gangway, like for a steamship. Half of it was already covered up on top with the soil. It led up to a window next to the smaller bathroom.'

The window that Bruno had fallen into. 'How high was this tunnel?'

'It was low. Less than three feet. You had to bend double.'

'Tell me something. What need was there for a tunnel?'

'Mr Spitaleri told us to build one. He wanted the foreman to check whether the pressure of the soil might damage the interior, letting in the damp and suchlike.'

'The foreman was Dipasquale?'

'Yessir.'

'And he came and checked?'

'Yessir. At the end of the first day. But he told us to keep working because everything was okay.'

'Did he also come on the last day?' It was Fazio, cutting in.

'Not in the morning when I was there. Maybe he came in the afternoon, but you'll have to ask Miccichè that.'

'You still haven't explained why you left early.'

'There wasn't much to do. Just closing a window with boards and plastic, taking apart the tunnel and smoothing the soil.'

'Did you notice if there was a trunk in the living room?'

'Yessir. The owner told us to put it down there, but I can't remember 'is name now. He asked me and someone called Smecca to carry it down.'

'Was it empty?'

'Yes.'

'Okay, thanks. You can go.'

Dalli Cardillo couldn't believe it. 'A good day to you all!' And he ran out.

'You know why Spitaleri didn't forewarn him of the interrogation and didn't tell him what to say?' asked Montalbano.

'No.'

'Because the man is shrewd. He knows Dalli Cardillo

is unaware of the murder. So he thought it was better if he came here with nothing to hide.'

*

Gaspare Miccichè was a fortyish redhead who was barely four feet eight inches tall. He had extremely long arms and bowed legs. He looked like a monkey. Surely if Darwin could have seen him, he would have hugged him for joy. Miccichè must have been able to enter the wooden tunnel practically standing up. He, too, was a bit nervous. 'You're making me miss a whole morning's work!'

'Mr Miccichè, do you have any idea why we summoned you here?'

'I not only have an idea, I *know* why because Mr Spitaleri talked to me before I came. It's about that fucking illegal apartment.'

'Didn't he tell you anything else?'

'Why? What else is there?'

'Listen, on that twelfth of October, which was your last day of work, at what time did you go home?'

'It wasn't the last day. I went back the next day too.'

'To do what?'

'What I didn't do the afternoon of the day before.'

'And what was that?'

'That afternoon, when I was getting down to work, Dipasquale, the foreman, arrived and told me not to dismantle the tunnel.'

'Why?'

'He said we'd better wait another day to see if there was any seepage. An' he also said the owner was coming in the afternoon to check things himself.'

'So what did you do?'

'What was I supposed to do? I left.'

'Go on.'

'That night, probably after nine o'clock, Dipasquale rang me to say I could take down the tunnel the following morning. So I boarded up the window and covered it with plastic, then dismantled the tunnel. I was just startin' to smoothe the ground when three men from the team arrived.'

'What team?'

'The ones that were supposed to remove the fencing from around the site. Then I went round the house twice with the grader and—'

'What's a grader?' asked Fazio.

'It's a machine like the one they use to make roads.'

'A steam-roller?'

'Yes, but smaller. When I'd finished, I went home.'

'With the grader?'

'No, the men from the team were supposed to take that away with their truck.'

'Do you remember whether you entered the apartment for any reason on the morning of the thirteenth?'

'Spitaleri asked me the same question. Nah, I didn't go in 'cause there wasn't any reason to.'

Had he gone in, he would have noticed at least the pool of blood in the living room. But he seemed sincere.

'Did you notice a trunk in there?'

'Yessir. It was the owner—'

'Yes, Mr Speciale asked for it to be brought down. Did you open it?'

'The trunk? No. I knew it was empty. Why would I open it?'

Without answering, Montalbano grabbed the printout, turned it over and handed it to him.

Miccichè looked at the photograph of the murdered girl, noticed the date of her disappearance and gave the printout back to the inspector. He looked genuinely stunned. 'What's that got to do with anything?'

It was Fazio who answered. 'If you had opened the trunk on the morning of the thirteenth, you would have found her inside it. Wrapped in plastic, with her throat slashed.'

Miccichè's reaction was not what they had expected. He shot to his feet, face turning purple, fists clenched, teeth bared. A wild animal. Montalbano was afraid he might jump on to the desk.

'Bastard!'

'Who?'

'Spitaleri! He knew and didn't tell me nothing! From the way he was talking to me, it's clear he wanted to get me into trouble!'

'Sit down and calm yourself. Why, in your opinion, would Spitaleri have wanted to get you into trouble?'

'To make you think it was me who killed that girl! When I went home that day, I left Dipasquale there! I don't know nothing about any of this!'

'Did you ever see this girl anywhere around the construction site?'

'Never!'

'When you stopped working on the afternoon of the twelfth, do you remember what you did?'

'How could I possibly remember? You're talking about six years ago!'

'Make an effort, Mr Miccichè. It's in your own interest,' said Fazio.

Miccichè was seized by another fit of rage. He leaped to his feet and, before Fazio could stop him, he ran to the door and butted it powerfully with his head. As Fazio was sitting him down by force, the door opened and a befuddled Catarella appeared. 'D'jou call for me, Chief?'

TEN

Between words and shoves, blandishments and brandishings of handcuffs, Fazio and Montalbano finally managed to get the unchained beast to calm down. Then, after some five minutes of good behaviour, head in his hands, concentrating as he tried to remember, Miccihé began to mutter: 'Wait a minute ... Wait a minute ...'

'The head-butt is bringing his memory back,' the inspector said to Fazio, under his breath.

'Wait a minute ... I think it was the same day that ... Yes ... Yes!' He leaped to his feet yet again, but Montalbano and Fazio were quick to jump on him and immobilize him. By now they'd learned the technique.

'But I just wanted to speak to my wife!'

'Well, if that's all ...' said the inspector.

Fazio held out the phone with the direct line for him. Miccihé dialled a number but was too nervous and got it wrong, reaching a grocery. He dialled again and got it wrong again.

'Let me do it for you.'

Miccichè told him the number, holding the receiver.

'Carmelina? 'S me. D'you remember six years ago when our Michilino broke 'is leg? Never mind why I'm asking you. Just say yes or no. Do you remember? You don't remember if it was six years ago? Think hard. Yes? And didn't it happen on the twelfth of October? Yes?'

He hung up.

'Now iss all comin' back to me. Since I got home early that day, I laid down and went to sleep. Then Carmelina woke me up, crying. Michilino 'ad fallen off 'is bike and broke 'is leg. So I took 'im to Montelusa 'ospital an' my wife came wit' me. We stayed at the 'ospital until that evening. You can check.'

'That's what we're going to do,' said Fazio. He exchanged a glance with Montalbano.

'For now you can go,' said the inspector.

'Thanks. I'm going to ram Spitaleri's teeth down his throat, even if it costs me my job!' And he left the room grinding his teeth.

'He acts as if he's escaped from a cage at the zoo,' commented Fazio.

'Why do you think Spitaleri didn't tell him anything about the murder?' the inspector asked.

'Because Spitaleri, having already left, had no way of knowing that Miccichè's kid broke his leg. He was convinced he didn't have an alibi.'

'So, in short, Miccichè got it right: Spitaleri wanted to set him up. But the question is, why?'

'Maybe because he thinks Dipasquale is involved. And Spitaleri cares more about Dipasquale, who probably knows a thing or two about him, than about some poor bastard like Miccichè.'

'Right.'

'What should I do? Call Dipasquale back in?'

'Are you harbouring suspicions about him?'

Thus the foreman also entered the game.

✻

Before going out to eat at the usual place, Enzo's trattoria, the inspector stopped in front of Catarella's cubby-hole, and the switchboard operator sprang to attention.

'At ease. Whatever happened with that fan?'

'Can't be found anywheres, Chief. Not even in Montelusa. They says they should have 'em in tree or four days' time.'

'Time enough for us to be properly roasted.'

Catarella accompanied him to the door and stood there watching him.

The blast of heat that came out of his car when Montalbano opened the door discouraged him from entering. Maybe it was better just to walk to Enzo's, which was about fifteen minutes away on foot, taking, naturally, the sides of the streets that were in the shade. He headed off.

'Chief! What – you goin' on foot?'

'Yes.'

'Wait a second.'

Catarella went back into the station and came out with a small green cap with a visor. He handed it to the inspector. 'Here, put this on to cover your head.'

'Oh, come on!'

'Chief! You're gonna get sunstricken!'

'Better sunstroke than looking like somebody going to the Pontida meetings.'

'Where you going, Chief?'

'Never mind.'

✱

After he'd been walking five minutes with his head down, he heard a voice: '*Vocumprà?*'

He looked up. An Arab selling sunglasses, straw hats, swimsuits. Next to his face, however, the man was holding a gadget that caught the inspector's attention, a sort of portable mini-fan that must have functioned with batteries. 'I'll take that,' he said, pointing to the fan.

'This is mine for me.'

'Haven't you got another?'

'No.'

'Come on, how much you want for it?'

'Fifty euros.'

Well, fifty euros was surely a lot.

'Let's make it thirty.'

'Forty.'

Montalbano paid him the forty euros, grabbed the little fan, and resumed walking, holding the gadget next to his face. He couldn't believe it: it actually cooled him very nicely.

Sitting down to eat, he wanted a light meal and had only a main course. It was thanks to the little fan that he was able to take his customary walk along the jetty and sit for a short while on the flat rock.

*

The mini-fan was endowed with a clamp, which allowed the inspector to attach it to the end of his desk. There was no doubt about it: the thing did provide a bit of relief in the overheated office.

'Catarella!'

'Behole the brillince o' man!' Catarella commented in admiration, upon seeing the little fan.

'Fazio here?'

'Yessir.'

'Tell him to come in.'

Fazio also congratulated him on the contraption.

'How much did you pay for it?'

'Ten euros.' He was embarrassed to admit he'd paid forty.

'Where'd you buy it? I want to get one myself.'

'Some Arab passing through. Unfortunately it was the only one he had.'

The telephone rang.

It was Dr Pasquano. The inspector turned on the speaker so Fazio could also hear.

'You all right, Montalbano?'

'Yes, why do you ask?'

'Well, considering the fact that you didn't bust my balls this morning, I was worried.'

'Did you perform the post-mortem?'

'Why else would I be phoning you? To hear your lovable, mellifluous voice?'

He must have discovered something important to have rung at all. 'Tell me about it.'

'Well, first of all, the girl had completely digested what she had eaten, but had not yet evacuated. Therefore she was killed either around six o'clock in the evening, or later, around eleven.'

'I think it was around six in the evening.'

'That's your business.'

'Is there anything else?'

The doctor didn't like saying what he was about to say. 'I was wrong.'

'About what?'

'The girl was a virgin. Beyond a shadow of a doubt.'

Montalbano and Fazio looked at each other in astonishment.

'What does that mean?' asked the inspector.

'You don't know what being a virgin means? Well, you must know that women who haven't yet—'

'You know perfectly well what I was referring to, Doctor.' Montalbano didn't feel like joking. Pasquano said nothing. 'If the girl died a virgin, it means the motive for the murder was not what we thought.'

'Did you know you're an Olympic champion?'

Montalbano looked dumbfounded. 'Explain yourself.'

'You're a champion in the hundred-metre sprint.'

'Why?'

'You're running too hard, my friend. Going too fast. It's not your job to reach an immediate conclusion. What's happening to you?'

What's happened to me is that I've grown old, thought the inspector, *and I want to reach a quick conclusion on a case that's been weighing on me.*

'So,' Pasquano resumed, 'I can confirm that, at the moment she was killed, the girl was in the position I said she was in.'

'Then explain to me why the murderer made her assume it, after having forced her to strip, if he wasn't going to screw her?'

'Since we haven't found any clothes, we can't know whether the killer forced her to strip before he killed her or stripped her himself afterwards. Anyway, the question of her clothes is unimportant, Montalbano.'

'You think so?'

'Of course! As unimportant as the fact that he wrapped up the body and put it in the trunk.'

'He didn't do it to hide her?'

'Do you know, Montalbano, you don't seem to be on very good form?'

'Maybe it's my age, Doctor.'

'What? The killer's going to take the trouble to put the body into a trunk while leaving a puddle of blood as big as a lake a couple of yards away?'

'Well, then, why, in your opinion, did he put her in the trunk?'

'With all the murders you've handled, you're asking me? To hide her from himself, my dear inspector, not from us! It's a sort of concrete, immediate repression of reality!'

Pasquano was right. How often had they come across amateur murderers who covered the victim's face, especially if it was a woman, with the first thing that came to hand, a rag, a towel, a sheet?

'You have to start with the only incontrovertible thing we've got,' the doctor continued, 'which is the girl's position when the killer cut her throat. If you concentrate a little, you'll see that—'

'I understand what you're trying to say.'

'If you finally understand, then tell me.'

'That maybe the killer, at the final moment, was no longer able to rape her, and so, in the throes of uncontrollable rage, he pulled out the knife—'

'Which, as they tell us in psychoanalysis, is a substitute for the penis. Very good.'

'Did I pass the exam?'

'Well, there may be another hypothesis,' Pasquano continued.

'What would that be?'

'That the killer sodomized her.'

'My God,' Fazio muttered.

'What?' The inspector rebelled. 'You fill my ears with idle chatter for half an hour and only deign to tell me at the end what you should have told me at the start?'

'It's just that I wasn't one hundred per cent sure. I wasn't able to establish the fact with any real certainty. Too much time has passed. But, based on a few very small signs, I would lean towards the affirmative. Mind you, I said I *would* lean. Conditional mood.'

'So, in short, you don't feel you could go from the conditional to another grammatical mood such as the present indicative?'

'Frankly, no.'

*

'It keeps getting worse and worse,' Fazio said bitterly, when the inspector hung up.

Montalbano remained pensive.

Fazio continued, 'Chief, do you remember when you said to me that when you catch the killer, you want to smash his face in?'

'Yes. And I reiterate the promise.'

'Can I join the party?'

'You're perfectly welcome to. Did you summon Dipasquale?'

'For six o'clock this evening, after he gets off work.'

As Fazio was leaving the room, the telephone rang again.

'Chief? Iss Proxecutor Dommaseo onna line.'

'Put him on,' said Montalbano. Then, to Fazio, 'You listen, too,' and he turned the speaker back on.

'Montalbano?'

'Judge?'

'I wanted to let you know that I've been to the Morreale home to give them the terrible news.' His voice was sorrowful, emotional.

'Very well done, sir.'

'It was awful, you know.'

'I can imagine.'

Tommaseo, however, wanted to tell him about his ordeal.

'Poor Signora Francesca, the mother, fainted. And the father, you wouldn't believe it, he was wandering about the house, talking to himself, and could hardly stand on his own two legs.'

Tommaseo was waiting for a comment from Montalbano, who obliged him. 'Poor things!'

'They'd been hoping, for all these years, that their daughter was still alive ... What's the expression? That hope ...'

'... is always the last thing to die,' Montalbano finished his sentence, obliging him again and cursing to himself for having had to use a cliché.

'That's so true, dear Montalbano.'

'So they were in no condition to identify the body.'

'No, it was identified, anyway! The dead girl is indeed Caterina Morreale!'

Montalbano and Fazio looked at each other in bewilderment. Why had Tommaseo suddenly pulled out this twittering voice that sounded as if it was coming from a little bird? It wasn't a pleasant matter he had dealt with, after all.

'I made a point of taking Adriana myself in my car,' Tommaseo continued.

'Wait a second. Who's Adriana?'

'What do you mean, "Who's Adriana"? Wasn't it you who told me the victim had a twin sister?'

Montalbano and Fazio looked at each other in disbelief. What was the man talking about? Maybe he was trying to turn the inspector's trick against him.

'You were right,' Tommaseo continued, his tone now of excitement, as if he'd just hit the jackpot. 'The girl is absolutely gorgeous!'

That explained the twittering.

'She studies medicine at Palermo — did you know? Mostly, she's a really strong girl with a lot of character, even though, after identifying the body, she had a little crisis and I had to comfort her.'

One could only imagine just how ready the good prosecutor had been to comfort her with every means at his disposal.

They said goodbye and hung up.

'But that's not possible!' said Fazio. 'You must have known there was a twin sister!'

'I swear to you I didn't. But it's an important thing to know. The victim probably confided in her. Could you telephone the Morreale home and ask if I can drop in tomorrow morning around ten?'

'Even though it's the fifteenth of August?'

'Where do you think they're going to go? They're in mourning.'

Fazio went out and came back five minutes later. 'Adriana herself answered the phone. She said it's probably better if you don't go to their place. Her parents are very upset and they're not in any condition to talk. She suggested she come here, to the station, at the same time tomorrow morning.'

✳

As the inspector was waiting for Dipasquale, he phoned the Aurora estate agency. 'Mr Callara? Montalbano here.'

'Is there any news, Inspector?'

'I haven't any. How about you?'

'Yes.'

'I bet you informed Signora Gudrun Speciale about the illegal floor we discovered.'

'Good guess! I called her the moment I had recovered a little from the shock I got opening that trunk. Damn my curiosity!'

'What can you do, Signor Callara? That's the way it goes, unfortunately.'

'I've always been curious. You know, once when I was a little boy—'

'But you were telling me about your phone call to Signora Gudrun . . .' The last thing he needed was Signor Callara's childhood memories.

'Ah, yes. But I didn't tell her about the poor girl who was killed.'

'You were right not to. What did Signora Gudrun decide?'

'She instructed me to take the necessary steps to obtain the amnesty and to send her the papers so she can sign them.'

'That sounds like the most sensible thing.'

'Yes, but then she faxed me a letter telling me that afterwards I'm to sell it. But do you know? I've got half a mind to buy that house myself. What do you think?'

'You're the estate agent. I'm sure you'll make the right decision. Goodbye.'

'Wait. There's more. When I was honestly advising her not to sell the house . . .' honestly in the sense that, if she sold it, Callara would lose his percentage of the rent '. . . she said that she didn't want to hear another word about it.'

'Did you ask her why?'

'Yes. She said she'd write to me about it. And just this morning a fax came in explaining why she wants to sell. I think it might be of interest to you.'

'To me?'

'Yes. She says her son, Ralf, is dead.'

'*What?*'

'Yes, they found his remains about two months ago.'

'His remains? You mean he died a long time ago?'

'Yes. Apparently he died on his way back to Cologne with Mr Speciale. She even sent a German newspaper clipping with a translation.'

'When can I see it?'

'This evening, when I close the office. I'll come to the station and drop it off with the man at the desk.'

And why had it taken them six years to find this other body, or what remained of it?

ELEVEN

The look Dipasquale gave the inspector as he entered the office was more surly than ever.

'Please sit down.'

'Will this take long?'

'As long as is needed. Mr Dipasquale, before we talk about the house in Pizzo, I'd like to ask you, now that I've got you here, where and how I might find the watchman of the construction site in Montelusa.'

'Are you still stuck on that damned business about the Arab? Inspector Lozupone himself—'

Montalbano pretended he hadn't heard his colleague's name. 'Tell me where I can find him. And give me his full name again. You told me last time, but I've forgotten it since I didn't write it down. Fazio, be sure to make a note of this.'

'Inspector.'

Not bad, as improvised theatre.

ANDREA CAMILLERI

'Inspector, I'll tell the watchman you want to talk to him. His name's Filiberto Attanasio.'

'I'm sorry, but how are you going to contact him when the site is closed?'

'He's got a mobile phone.'

'Please give me the number.'

'It doesn't work. The other night ... the other day, I mean, it fell on the ground and broke.'

'Okay, so tell him in person.'

'All right, but I should warn you, he won't be able to come for two or three days.'

'Why not?'

'He's had an attack of malaria.'

They must have scared the watchman pretty comprehensively.

'Tell you what, when he's feeling better, tell him to give us a call. Now, back to us. I asked you to come in because this morning I questioned two masons, named Dalli Cardillo and Miccichè, who worked on the house in Pizzo—'

'Inspector, don't waste your breath. I know exactly what happened.'

'Who told you?'

'Spitaleri. Miccichè went into his office acting as if he was out of his mind and punched him so hard he gave him a bloody nose. He was convinced Spitaleri wanted to set him up. The man oughta be caged with wild animals!

148

Well, he can start begging now, 'cause he won't find it easy to get any more work as a mason.'

'Spitaleri's not the only builder in town,' said Fazio.

'Maybe, but all it'll take is a word from me or Spitaleri—'

'To have him on the streets?'

'You said it.'

'I shall make a note of what you just told me and take proper action,' said Montalbano.

'What does that mean?' asked Dipasquale, alarmed. More than the threatening tone, what frightened him most was the inspector's use of correct Italian.

'It means that you said, in our presence, that you will see to it that Miccichè remains unemployed. You threatened a witness.'

'Witness? What witness? I think you mean witless!'

'You will not speak to me in that fashion!'

'Anyway, if I'm threatening him, it's not for what he said here but for punching Spitaleri!'

Quick and clever, was the foreman.

'For now, let's not get away from the subject. Spitaleri told us that work on the Pizzo house ended on the twelfth of October. Which you confirmed. But the work didn't end until the morning of the following day, as we found out from Miccichè.'

'What's the difference?'

'That's for us to decide. Spitaleri could not have

known that the work had carried over into the next day because he'd already left. But did you know?'

'Yes.'

'In fact, wasn't it you yourself who made the decision to prolong it?'

'Yes.'

'Why didn't you tell us?'

'It slipped my mind.'

'Are you sure?'

'Anyway, last time I came in, you didn't tell me about the girl that was killed.'

He was trying to counterattack, the idiot.

'Dipasquale, we're not here to play "you tell me one thing, and I'll tell you another". At any rate, when you walked in you already knew, of course, about the dead girl, because Spitaleri had told you about her. And yet you acted as if nothing had happened.'

'What was I supposed to say? Nothing.'

'No, no! You did say something.'

'What?'

'You tried to create an alibi for yourself. You said that four days before the work in Pizzo was completed, Spitaleri sent you to Fela to start on a new site. So why is it that, on the eleventh and twelfth of October, in the afternoon, you were at Pizzo and not in Fela?'

Dipasquale didn't even try to come up with an excuse. 'Inspector, you've got to understand. I was really scared when Spitaleri told me about the dead body so I made up that story about being sent to Fela. But I knew that sooner or later you'd find out it was a lie.'

'Then tell us exactly what happened.'

'Well, at eleven o'clock I went into that damned apartment. I wanted to see if it was damp or if there was any seepage. I even went into the living room, but I didn't see nothing strange.'

'What about the next day, the twelfth?'

'I went back there in the afternoon. I told Miccichè not to dismantle the tunnel. Then he left and I stayed another half-hour to wait for Mr Speciale.'

'Did you go inside to check everything?'

'Yessir. An' everything was in order.'

'In the living room, too?' asked Fazio.

'In the living room, too.'

'And then?'

'Finally Mr Speciale arrived.'

'How did he come?'

'By car. He'd rented it when he got here.'

'Was his stepson with him?'

'Yessir.'

'What time was it?'

'Probably around four.'

'Did you go downstairs?'

'All three of us.'

'How could you see?'

'I had a powerful torch. And Mr Speciale had one, too. Mr Speciale checked everything very closely. He's a very fussy man. A stickler. Then I asked him if we could close up the passage and level the ground, and he said okay. He gave one last look, and then we went outside, Mr Speciale and me. We said goodbye, and I left.'

'What about Ralf?'

'The boy asked his stepfather for the torch and stayed downstairs.'

'To do what?'

'Dunno. He just liked being underground. He looked at all the wrapped-up window frames and laughed. Didn't I tell you he was crazy?'

'So, when you left, Speciale and Ralf stayed behind in Pizzo?'

'That's where I left 'em. Anyway, Mr Speciale had the keys to the apartment, which was habitable.'

'Do you remember more or less what time it was when you left?'

'Around five.'

'Why did you wait until nine o'clock that night to inform Miccichè that he could take down the tunnel?'

'I phoned him at least three times, and there was never any answer. I didn't reach him till the evening.'

It made sense. Miccichè and his wife had spent the afternoon and early evening at Montelusa hospital.

'What did you do after you left Pizzo?'

Dipasquale gave a slight chuckle. 'You want an alibi?'

'You'll be better off if you've got one.'

'I have. I went into Mr Spitaleri's office. He was supposed to be ringing us – the secretary and me – between six and eight o'clock.'

'But he hadn't landed in Bangkok,' said Fazio.

'Of course not. But the flight was making a stop in some place whose name I can't remember. Spitaleri knows the route. He goes to those places often.'

'Did he ring?'

'Yes.'

'Was it an important phone call?'

'It was pretty important. It was about a government contract we was supposed to be getting. If we got it, then I'd have to deal with a few things.'

Such as, for example, doling out to the Sinagras, the Cuffaros, the mayor and anyone else in charge the wads of money they had coming to them, thought the inspector. But he didn't say anything.

'So, I'm curious to know, did you get it?' asked Fazio.

'By the twelfth they hadn't decided. They decided on the fourteenth.'

'In your favour?' Fazio asked again.

'Yes.'

How could you go wrong?

'And did you tell Spitaleri?'

'Yes, the following day. We rang him at his hotel in Bangkok.'

'Who's we?'

'The secretary and me. Anyway, to conclude, if you want to know what happened at Pizzo after I left, you'll have to call Mr Speciale in Germany.'

'He's dead. Didn't you know?'

'What? Heart-attack, was it?'

'No, he fell down the stairs at his home.'

'Well, you can always ask Ralf.'

'He's dead, too. I found out half an hour ago.'

Dipasquale staggered.

'*Whaaat?*'

'He got on the train with his stepfather but never arrived in Cologne. He must have fallen off.'

'So that house in Pizzo is cursed!' the foreman said, disturbed.

You're telling me! Montalbano thought. He grabbed the printout with the photo from his desk and handed it to him. Dipasquale took it, looked at the photograph, and his face turned flaming red.

'Do you know her?'

'Yes. She's one of the twin girls who lived in the last house on the dirt road at Pizzo, before the one we built.'

So that was why the missing-persons report had been made in Fiacca. At the time Montereale had fallen within that jurisdiction.

'This is the girl who was killed?' asked Dipasquale, still holding the printout in his hand.

'Yes.'

'I'm positive that . . .'

'Speak.'

'You remember what I told you last time? This is the girl Ralf chased around naked and Spitaleri saved.' Suddenly Dipasquale realized he'd made a mistake. Talking without thinking, he'd dragged Spitaleri into it. He tried to put things right. 'Or maybe not. In fact, there's no "maybe" about it. I got it wrong. This is the twin sister, I'm sure of it.'

'Did you see the twins often?'

'Often, no. Now and then. There was no way to get to Pizzo without driving past their house.'

'How come Miccichè said he'd never seen her before?'

'Inspector, the masons would come to the site at seven in the morning when the girls were still asleep, I'm sure. An' they got off work at five thirty, when the girls were still on the beach. But me, I went back and forth, to and from the site.'

'How about Spitaleri?'

'He came less often.'

'Thanks, you can go,' Montalbano concluded.

'What do you make of Dipasquale's alibi?' Fazio asked, after the foreman had left.

'It could be true or it could be false. It rests entirely on a phone call from Spitaleri that we don't know was ever made.'

'We could ask the secretary.'

'Really? The secretary will do and say exactly what Spitaleri tells her to do and say. Otherwise she'll find

herself one hundred per cent sacked. And with the short-
age of work there is, these days, I don't imagine she'll
want to jeopardize her job.'

'I get the feeling we're not making any progress.'

'I've got the same feeling. Tomorrow we'll hear what
Adriana has to say.'

'Would you explain to me why you want to talk to
Filiberto?'

'But I don't want to talk to him. I just wanted to see
what Dipasquale's reaction would be. Whether he had any
suspicions about us being the two who paid Filiberto a
visit the other night.'

'It looks to me as if they haven't thought of us.'

'Sooner or later they'll come to that conclusion.'

'And what will they do then?'

'In my opinion, they won't show their hand. Spitaleri
will complain to the little friends who protect him, and
they'll do something.'

'Like what?'

'Fazio, we'll wait for them to come and beat us up,
and then we'll start crying.'

'Okay,' Fazio began, 'I'm going—'

A bang as loud as a cannon-shot interrupted him. It
was the door slamming against the wall. Catarella was still
standing there with one arm raised, his fist closed, and
holding an envelope in his other hand.

'Sorry 'bout the noise, Chief. Somebuddy just now
brought a litter.'

'Give it to me and get out of here before I shoot you.'

It was a big envelope, and in it were two faxes sent from Germany and addressed to Callara's agency.

'Stay and listen, Fazio. This contains the news of Ralf's death. Callara sent it.'

Montalbano began reading aloud.

Dear Sir,

Three months ago, while reading a newspaper, I happened to notice a news item, of which I am herewith sending you a copy with accompanying translation.

I immediately felt, perhaps by maternal instinct, that those wretched remains must belong to my poor Ralf, for whom I have been waiting all these long years.

I asked that a comparison be made between the unknown man's DNA and my son's. It was not at all easy to obtain consent for such a test; I had to insist for a long time.

Finally, a few days ago, the result was sent to me.

The data correspond perfectly. Beyond a shadow of a doubt, those remains belong to my late son Ralf.

Since no trace of clothing was found, the police maintain that Ralf got up in the night to go to the lavatory during his return home from Italy by train, accidentally opened the outside door, and fell out.

That house in Sicily has brought us nothing but misfortune. It led to the death of both my son Ralf and my husband Angelo, who after his trip to Sicily, and certainly after Ralf's disappearance, was no longer the same man.

For this reason, I would like to sell the house.

Some time in the next few days I will fax you copies of all the documents related to the house's construction: the blueprints, the permit, the Land Registry plan, and the contracts with Spitaleri Enterprises. You will need these for the amnesty request as well as for the future sale.

Gudrun Walser

The translation of the news item went as follows:

Remains of Unidentified Man Found

The day before yesterday, following a fire that broke out in the dense brush on a railway embankment some twenty kilometres outside Cologne, the remains of a human body were discovered half-buried in a dip in the ground by firemen who had rushed to the scene to control the flames. No certification of the man's identity could be made, however, because no clothing or documents were found in the vicinity.

The post-mortem revealed beyond doubt that the remains belonged to a young man, and that the death dated from at least five years ago.

'This fall from the train doesn't convince me,' said Fazio.

'Or me. The police say Ralf got up to go to the lavatory. Would he have done that naked? What if he'd run into someone in the corridor?'

'So, what do you think?'

'Bah. It's all guesswork, as you know. We'll never have

any proof or confirmation. Maybe Ralf spotted a pretty girl on the train and decided to strip off and try to kiss her, as Dipasquale said he liked to do. And maybe he ran into her husband, father or boyfriend, who threw him out of the train.'

'That sounds like a bit of a stretch to me.'

'There's another possible explanation. Suicide.'

'For what reason?'

'Let's make an argument based on the fact that, on the afternoon of the twelfth of October, Angelo Speciale and his stepson remained in Pizzo alone, as Dipasquale says. Say Angelo goes out onto the terrace to enjoy the sunset while Ralf goes for a walk in the direction of the Morreale house. Don't forget that Dipasquale told us that Ralf had once tried to grab Rina. He happens to run into her, and this time doesn't want to let her get away. He threatens the girl with a knife and forces her to go with him into the underground apartment. And that's where the tragedy occurs. Ralf wraps up the girl's body, puts it in the trunk, takes her clothes, hides them in the house, then goes out on the terrace to keep Angelo company. The stepfather, however, finds the girl's clothes, maybe on their last day there. Maybe they were even stained with her blood when he killed her.'

'But hadn't he made her take her clothes off?'

'We don't know. It's possible he only stripped her afterwards. There was no need for her to be completely naked for him to do what he wanted to do.'

'So, how does it end?'

'It ends as follows: during the train ride back to Germany, Angelo forces Ralf to confess to the murder. And, after confessing, the boy kills himself by jumping off the train. But I can give you a variant, if you like.'

'What?'

'Angelo throws him off the train, killing the monster.'

'Pretty far-fetched, Chief.'

'Whatever the case, don't forget that Signora Gudrun wrote that when her husband got back to Cologne, he said he never wanted to leave again. Something must therefore have happened to him.'

'You're damn right something happened to him. The poor man woke up the next morning in his sleeping car and his stepson was gone!'

'In short, you don't see Speciale as a murderer?'

'No.'

'But in Greek tragedy—'

'We're in Vigàta, Chief, not Greece.'

'Tell me the truth: do you like the story or don't you?'

'It might do for TV.'

TWELVE

It had been a long day, made longer by the August heat. The inspector felt a little tired. But he had no lack of appetite.

When he opened the oven, he was disappointed not to find anything. But when he opened the refrigerator, he saw a salad of calamari, celery and tomatoes that still needed to be dressed with olive oil and lemon. Adelina had wisely prepared him a dish to be eaten cold.

A mild, newborn breeze was circulating on the veranda. It was too feeble to move the dense mass of heat that was holding out as night fell, but it was better than nothing.

He took off his clothes, put on his trunks, ran down to the water and dived in. He went for a long swim, in broad, slow strokes. Returning to shore, he went into the house, set the little table on the veranda, and began to eat. When he had finished, he still felt hungry, so he prepared a plate of green olives, cured black *passuluna* olives, and *caciocavallo* cheese that called for — indeed demanded — good wine.

The light breeze on the veranda had matured from infancy to adolescence and was making itself felt.

He decided to seize this favourable moment when his thoughts weren't log-jammed by the heat, and consider rationally the investigation he had on his hands. He cleared the little table of dishes, cutlery and glasses, and replaced them with a few sheets of paper.

Since he didn't like to take notes, he decided to write himself a letter, as he sometimes did.

Dear Montalbano,

I am forced to point out that, either from the onset of a senile second childhood or because of the intense heat of the last few days, your thoughts have lost all their lustre and become extremely opaque and slow-moving. You had a chance to see this for yourself during your dialogue with Dr Pasquano, who easily got the better of you in that exchange.

Pasquano presented two hypotheses concerning the fact that the killer took away the girl's clothes: one, it was an irrational act; and two, the killer took them because he's a fetishist. Both hypotheses are plausible.

But there is a third possibility. It occurred to you as you were talking to Fazio, and that is that the killer took the clothes because they were stained with blood. Stained with the blood that had spouted from the girl's throat as he was killing her.

But things may well have gone differently. You need to take a step back.

Neither when you discovered the body yourself, nor when you made Callara discover it officially, did you see the giant bloodstain near the french windows, and you didn't see it for the simple reason that it wasn't visible to the naked eye. The Forensics team only noticed it because they used luminol.

If the killer had left the big stain exactly as it had formed on the floor, some traces of dried blood would have remained on the tiles, even six years later. Whereas, in fact, nothing was found.

What does this mean?

It means that the man, after killing the girl, wrapping her up and sticking her in the trunk, used her clothes to wipe up, however superficially, the pool of blood. He dampened them with a little water, since the taps were in working order, then put them in a little plastic bag that he'd found there or brought with him.

Now the question is: Why didn't he get rid of the clothes by simply throwing the bag on top of the corpse?

And the answer is: Because in order to do that, he would have had to reopen the trunk.

And that was impossible for him, because it would have meant having the reality he had already begun to repress thrown back in his face. Pasquano is right: he hid the body not to stop us seeing it but to stop himself seeing it.

There's still another important question. It's already been asked, but it's worth repeating: Was it necessary to kill the girl? And, if so, why?

As for the 'why', Pasquano hinted at the possibility of blackmail, or a fit of temporary insanity from rage at finding himself suddenly impotent.

My answer is: Yes, it was necessary. But for only one, completely different, reason.

The following: the girl knew her aggressor well.

The killer must have forced the girl to enter the underground apartment with him, and once she was down there, her fate was sealed. For if the man had left her alive, she would surely have accused him of rape or attempted rape. Thus, when the killer took her underground, he already knew that, in addition to raping her, he would also have to murder her. On this point, there could be no more doubt. Premeditated murder.

Then comes the mother of all questions: Who was the killer? One must proceed by process of elimination.

It definitely could not have been Spitaleri. Even though you can't stand the man, and even though you'll try to screw him on some other charge, there is one incontrovertible fact: on the afternoon of the twelfth, Spitaleri was not in Pizzo but on a flight to Bangkok. And bear in mind that, for Spitaleri, a girl of Rina's age is already too mature for his tastes.

Miccichè has an alibi: he spent the afternoon at Montelusa hospital. You can have this verified, if you like, but it will be a waste of time.

Dipasquale says he has an alibi. He left Pizzo at around five in the afternoon and went to Spitaleri's office to receive his boss's phone call. At nine p.m., he spoke to Miccichè. But he didn't tell us what he did after going to Spitaleri's office. He said he and his boss had agreed he would ring between six and eight o'clock. Let's say for the sake of argument that the phone call comes in at six thirty. Dipasquale leaves the office and happens to run into

Rina. He knows her, asks her if she wants a lift back to Pizzo. The girl accepts and ... That leaves Dipasquale plenty of time to telephone Micciché by nine.

Ralf. He stays behind in Pizzo with his stepfather after Dipasquale has gone. He knows Rina, has already tried to assault her. What if things actually did happen in the way you told Fazio? The mystery of his death remains, and could be linked in some way to his guilt. But accusing Ralf would be, to all intents and purposes, an act of faith. He's dead, his stepfather is dead. Neither could tell us what happened.

In conclusion: Dipasquale should be the number-one suspect. But you're not convinced.

A big hug and take care.

Yours, Salvo

He was taking off his trunks, getting ready to go to bed when, all of a sudden, he felt like talking to Livia. He dialled the number of her mobile phone. It rang for a long time, but nobody answered.

Why not? Was Massimiliano's boat so big that Livia couldn't hear her phone? Or was she too engaged, too busy doing other things to answer it?

He was about to hang up in anger when he heard Livia's voice. 'Hello? Who is it?'

What did she mean, "who is it"? Couldn't she read the caller's number on the display or whatever the hell it was called? 'It's Salvo.'

'Oh, it's you.'

Not disappointed. Indifferent.

'What were you doing?'

'Sleeping.'

'Where?'

'On the deck. I fell asleep without realizing it. It's all so peaceful, so beautiful . . .'

'Where are you?'

'We're sailing towards Sardinia.'

'And where's Massimiliano?'

'He was beside me when I fell asleep. Now I think he's—'

He cut her off, pulling out the plug.

And what was that fucking idiot Massimiliano doing there? Singing her a lullaby?

He went to bed with his hair standing on end.

And it took the hand of God to fall asleep.

*

In vain he went for a swim after waking; in vain he got into the shower, which should have been cold but was actually hot because the water in the tanks on the roof was so torrid you could have boiled pasta in it; in vain he dressed as lightly as possible.

The moment he set foot outside the house, he had to admit that it was no use. The heat was a fiery blaze.

He went back into the house, shoved a shirt, underpants and pair of trousers as thin as onion skin in a shopping bag, and left.

He arrived at the station with his shirt drenched in sweat and his underpants all of a piece with the skin of his arse, so tightly were they sticking.

Catarella tried to stand up and salute but couldn't manage it, falling lifelessly back into his chair. 'Ah, Chief, Chief! I'm dying! 'S the devil, this heat!'

'Deal with it!'

He slipped into the cloakroom. He took off all his clothes, washed himself, pulled out the fresh shirt, underpants and trousers, got dressed, returned to his office and turned on the mini-fan.

'Catarella!'

'Comin', Chief.'

He was closing the shutters when Catarella entered. 'Your ord...' He trailed off, braced himself against the desk with his left hand, and brought his right hand to his forehead, closing his eyes. He looked like an illustration in a nineteenth-century acting manual for the expression 'shock and dismay'. 'Jesus, Jesus, Jesus...' he said in litany.

'Cat, are you ill?'

'Jesus, Chief, whatta scare! The heat's got into my head!'

'But what's wrong?'

'Nuttin', Chief, go 'head 'n' talk. I feel fine. My ears are workin' great, iss my eyes got me seein' tings.' And he didn't move from his position: eyes shut tight, hand on his forehead.

'In the cloakroom there are some clothes I've just changed out of . . .'

'Ya changed clothes?' said Catarella. He looked relieved, lowered his hand from his forehead and eyed Montalbano as if he'd never seen him before. 'So ya changed clothes!'

'Yes, Cat, I changed clothes. What's so weird about that?'

'Nuttin' weird, Chief, it was jes' a misunnerstannin'! I seen ya come in dressed one ways 'n' then I seen ya dressed anutter ways 'n' so I tought I was lahuccinating cuzza the heat. 'S a good ting ya changed clothes!'

'Go and get those clothes and hang them out in the courtyard to dry.'

'I'll take care of it straight aways.'

On his way out, he was about to close the door but the inspector stopped him. 'Leave it open, so there's a little draught.'

The direct line rang. It was Mimì Augello. 'How are you, Salvo? I tried you at home but there was no answer, and then I remembered that you don't give a shit about the fifteenth of August so—'

'You were right, Mimì. How's Beba? And the little one?'

'Salvo, don't ask. The baby's had a fever since the moment we got here. The upshot is we haven't had a single moment of holiday. Only yesterday did the fever pass, finally. And tomorrow I'm supposed to be back at work . . .'

'I understand, Mimì. As far as I'm concerned, you can stay another week if you want.'

'Really?'

'Really. Say hi to Beba for me and give your son a kiss.'

Five minutes later, the other telephone rang. 'Aaah, Chief! Iss the c'mishner says he emergently needs to—'

'Tell him I'm not in.'

'And where should I tell him you went to?'

'The dentist's.'

'You got a toothache?'

'No, Cat, it's the excuse I want you to give him.'

The c'mishner was harrying him even on 15 August.

*

As he was signing some papers that Fazio explained had been piling up for a few months, he happened to look up. In the corridor he saw Catarella coming towards his office. But what was it that looked so strange about the way he was walking? The inspector knew the answer as soon as he'd asked the question.

Catarella, as he walked, was dancing. That was it. Dancing. He was on tiptoe, arms stretched away from his body, hinting at a half-pirouette every few steps. Had the heat indeed gone to his head? As he entered the office, the inspector noticed he was keeping his eyes closed. *O matre santa*, what had happened to him? Was he sleepwalking? 'Catarella!'

Catarella, who had come up to the desk, opened his eyes, stunned. He had a faraway look. 'Huh?' he said.

'What's got into you?'

'Ah, Chief, Chief! There's a girl here you gotta see with your eyes! She's the spittin' image of the poor girl that got killed! *Mamma mia*, she's so beauty-full! I never seen anyting like 'er.'

It was Beauty, with a capital B, that had given Catarella's step a dancing lilt, his gaze a dreamy look.

'Send her in and inform Fazio.'

He saw her coming from the end of the corridor.

Catarella walked in front of her, literally bent over, making a bizarre movement with his hand as if he was cleaning the floor where she was about to set her foot. Or maybe he was unrolling an invisible carpet.

And as the girl approached and her features, eyes and hair colour became more and more distinct, the inspector slowly stood up, feeling himself drowning happily in a sort of blissful nothingness.

> Head of pale gold
> With eyes of sky blue,
> Who gave you the power
> To make me no longer myself?

It was a quatrain by Pessoa, singing in his head. He collected himself and emerged from the nothingness to return to his office.

But he had succeeded only by dealing himself a low,

malicious blow as painful as it was necessary: *she's young enough to be your daughter.*

'I'm Adriana Morreale.'

'Salvo Montalbano.'

'Sorry I'm late, but . . .'

She was half an hour late.

They shook hands. The inspector's was a little sweaty, Adriana's was dry. She was cool and fresh and smelled of soap, as if she wasn't coming in from outside but had just stepped out of the shower.

'Please sit down. Catarella, did you inform Fazio?'

'Huh?'

'Did you inform Fazio?'

'Straight aways, Chief.'

He walked out with his head turned backwards, gawping at the girl for as long as he could.

Montalbano took the opportunity to observe her, and she let herself be observed.

She must have been used to it.

Jeans clinging to very long legs, low-cut light blue blouse, sandals. One point in her favour: her navel was not exposed. She was clearly not wearing a bra. And there wasn't a trace of makeup on her face. She had done nothing to make herself beautiful. What else could she do, after all?

After a good look at her, one could see a few differences with respect to the photograph of her twin sister, due, no doubt, to the fact that Adriana was six years older, and they couldn't have been easy years. The eyes had the same shape and colour but the innocence that shone in Rina's gaze was gone from Adriana's. And the girl sitting in front of the inspector also had a faint line at each corner of her mouth.

'Do you live with your parents in Vigàta?'

'No. I quickly realized that my presence was a source of suffering to them. They couldn't help but see my missing sister in me. So, when I enrolled at the university – I'm studying medicine – I bought an apartment in Palermo. But I come back often. I don't like to leave them alone for long.'

'What year are you in?'

'I've signed up for the third.'

Fazio came in and, although he'd been prepared by Catarella, his eyes popped out the moment he saw her. 'Hi, my name's Fazio.'

'I'm Adriana Morreale.'

'Perhaps it'd be best if you shut the door,' said the inspector.

Once news got round that a beautiful girl was in his office, in five minutes the hallway would be jammed with more traffic than a city street at rush-hour.

Fazio closed the door and sat down in the other chair in front of the inspector's desk. But this brought him face to face with the girl. He decided to pull back until he was off to one side of the desk, slightly closer to Montalbano.

'Forgive me for not allowing you to come to my home, Inspector.'

'Not at all. I understand perfectly.'

'Thank you. You can ask me all the questions you want.'

'Prosecutor Tommaseo told us it was you who had to perform the painful task of identifying the body. I'm very sorry, but my job requires me, and I want to apologize for it now, to ask you certain questions that—'

Then Adriana did something that neither Fazio nor Montalbano was expecting. She threw her head back and laughed. 'My God, you talk like he does! You and Tommaseo use exactly the same words! Do they make you take a special course?'

Montalbano felt at once offended and liberated. Offended for having been compared to Tommaseo, and liberated because he realized the girl didn't like formality. It made her laugh.

'I told you,' Adriana continued, 'to ask me all the questions you want. You don't have to walk on eggshells. It doesn't seem your style.'

'Thanks,' said Montalbano.

Fazio, too, appeared relieved.

'You, unlike your parents, always imagined your sister was dead, is that right?' Just like that, straight to the point, the way she wanted and the way everyone preferred.

Adriana gave him an admiring look. 'Yes, but I didn't imagine it. I knew it.'

ANDREA CAMILLERI

Montalbano and Fazio both, at the same time, leaped slightly out of their chairs.

'You *knew*? Who told you?'

'Nobody actually told me directly.'

'So how did you know?'

'My body told me. And I've trained my body never to lie to me.'

THIRTEEN

What did she mean?

'Could you please explain to me how ... ?'

'It's not easy. It's because we were identical twins. The phenomenon is hard to describe, but it used to happen to us now and then. A sort of confused, long-distance communication of emotion.'

'Go on.'

'I will, but first I want to make clear that I'm not talking about the sort of phenomenon where if one of us skinned her knee, the other, even if she was far away, would feel pain in the same knee. Nothing like that. If anything, it was more like transmitting a strong emotion. For example, on the day Grandma died, Rina was there but I was in Fela playing with my cousins. All of a sudden, I was overwhelmed by such sadness that I started crying for no apparent reason. It was as though Rina had transmitted her emotions at that moment.'

'Did this happen all the time?'

'No.'

'Where were you the day your sister didn't come home?'

'I'd left just that morning, on the twelfth, to see my aunt and uncle in Montelusa. I was supposed to stay with them for two or three days, but I came home late that evening after Papa called my uncle to tell him Rina had disappeared.'

'Listen ... on the afternoon, or the evening, of the twelfth ... was there anything ... you know ... any sort of "communication", between your sister and you?'

Montalbano was having trouble formulating his question. Adriana helped him out. 'Yes, there was. At seven thirty-eight in the evening. I instinctively glanced at my watch.'

Montalbano and Fazio looked at each other.

'What happened?'

'I had a little room of my own at my uncle's and aunt's place, and I was alone, choosing what to wear that evening because we'd been invited to dinner by some friends ... Just then I had this feeling, but not like the other times. It was sort of physical. She was strangled, wasn't she?'

She was close. 'Not exactly. What did Prosecutor Tommaseo tell you?'

'Prosecutor Tommaseo said she'd been murdered, but he didn't specify how. He also told me where she'd been found.'

'When you went to the morgue to identify the body—'

'I asked them to show me only the feet. That was enough. The big toe on her right—'

'I know. But afterwards, didn't you ask Tommaseo how she died?'

'Inspector, my only concern after identifying the body was to liberate myself as quickly as possible from Tommaseo. He started to console me by patting me lightly on the back, but then his hand was sliding downwards, too far downwards. It's not like me to play the prude, far from it, but that man was a real nuisance. What was he supposed to tell me?'

'That your sister's throat was slashed.'

Adriana turned pale and her hand flew to her own. 'Oh, my God!' she whispered.

'Can you tell me what you felt at that moment?'

'A violent pain in my neck. For a minute that seemed like for ever, I couldn't breathe. But at the time it didn't occur to me that the pain might be related to something that was happening to my sister.'

'What did you think it was related to?'

'You see, Inspector, Rina and I were identical, but only physically. We were completely different in the way we thought, the way we behaved. Rina would never have done anything against the rules, not even the tiniest thing, but I, on the other hand, would. In fact, I rather liked to, from around that time. I started smoking on the sly. And that day I'd had three cigarettes in a row, keeping the window in my little bedroom open. For no reason, just for the pleasure of doing it. So when I felt that pain in my throat, I naturally thought it was because of the cigarettes.'

'And when did you realize it had to do with your sister?'

'Immediately afterwards.'

'Why?'

'I connected it to another thing that had happened to me just a few minutes earlier.'

'Can you tell us what that was?'

'I'd rather not.'

'Did you tell your parents about – about this contact with your sister?'

'No. This is the first time I've talked about it.'

'Why didn't you tell them?'

'Because it was a secret between Rina and me. We had sworn never to tell anyone.'

'Did you and your sister confide a lot in each other?'

'How could we not?'

'Did you tell each other everything?'

'Everything.'

Now came the most difficult questions. 'Would you like something to drink from the cafe downstairs? I can send someone to fetch it.'

'No, thanks. We can continue.'

'Don't you have to go home? Are your parents alone?'

'Thanks, but please don't worry. I asked a friend to look after them. She's a nurse, so they're in good hands.'

'Did Rina ever mention to you that anyone, during those final weeks, was bothering her?'

Adriana did the same thing as before. She threw her head back and laughed. 'Would you believe me, Inspector, if I told you that there wasn't a single man, from when we were thirteen, who didn't "bother" us, as you put it? I found it rather amusing, but Rina hated it and got very angry.'

'There was one specific incident that was brought to our attention, and which we'd like to know more about.'

'You're talking about Ralf.'

'You knew him?'

'It would have been hard not to. While his stepfather's house was being built, he came round to our place every other day.'

'What did he do?'

'Well, he would come and then he would hide, waiting for our parents to go into town or down to the beach. Then, after we got up, he would spy on us through the window as we were having breakfast. I thought it was funny. Sometimes I would throw him little pieces of bread, as if he was a dog. He liked that game. Rina couldn't stand him.'

'Was he sane?'

'You must be joking. He was out of his mind. One day something more serious happened. I was alone in the house. The upstairs shower wasn't working so I used the one downstairs. When I came out, there he was, right in front of me, completely naked.'

'How did he get in?'

'Through the front door. I'd thought it was closed, but it had been left ajar. It was the first time Ralf came into the house. I didn't even have a towel round me. He looked at me with a dog-like expression and asked me to give him a kiss.'

'What did he say?'

'He said, "Please, won't you give me a kiss?"'

'Weren't you afraid?'

'No. That isn't the kind of thing that frightens me.'

'So, what was the upshot?'

'I decided to humour him. I kissed him, very lightly, but on the lips. He put a hand on my breast and caressed it, then he bowed his head and collapsed into a chair. I ran upstairs and got dressed, and when I went down again he'd gone.'

'Didn't you think he might try to rape you?'

'Not for a second.'

'Why not?'

'Because I realized immediately that he was impotent. I could tell even from the way he looked at me. And I had my confirmation when I kissed him and he caressed me. He didn't have a ... well, any visible reaction.'

Deep inside his ears the inspector distinctly heard the sound of his hypotheses falling noisily to pieces. Ralf forcing the girl to go into the underground apartment, raping her, killing her, then killing himself or being forced to kill himself ... He exchanged a glance of dismay with Fazio, who looked befuddled.

Then he gazed admiringly at Adriana. How many girls had he met who could say things as straightforwardly as she? 'Did you tell Rina about this incident?'

'Of course.'

'So why did she run away when Ralf tried to kiss her? Didn't she know he was harmless?'

'Inspector, I already told you that, as far as this sort of thing was concerned, we were very different. Rina wasn't afraid, she just felt deeply offended by it, and that was why she ran away.'

'I was told that Spitaleri, the developer—'

'Yes, he happened to drive past at that moment. He saw Rina running away and Ralf chasing her, naked. He stopped, got out of his car and punched Ralf so hard that he fell over. Then he bent over him, pulled a knife out of his pocket and told him that if he ever bothered my sister again he'd kill him.'

'And then?'

'Then he told her to get into his car and drove her home.'

'Did he stay long?'

'Rina said she gave him a cup of coffee.'

'Do you know whether Spitaleri and your sister ever saw each other again?'

ANDREA CAMILLERI

'Yes.'

At that moment the telephone rang. 'Aah, Chief, Chief! The c'mishner wants to talk to you emergently straight aways and poissonally in poisson.'

'But why didn't you tell him I was still at the dentist's?'

'I made an attemptation to tell 'im you's still out, but he said, the c'mishner said, I mean, not to tell 'im you's still at the dennist's and so I said you's here in the office in poisson.'

'Put him on the line in Augello's office, and I'll pick it up in there.' He stood up. 'You'll have to excuse me, Adriana. I'll be back as soon as I can. Fazio, you come with me.'

In Mimì's office, into which the sun shone directly, the heat was stifling. 'Hello? What can I do for you, Commissioner?'

'Montalbano! Have you any idea?'

'Of what?'

'What? You don't have any idea?'

'Of what?'

'You didn't even deign to answer!'

'Answer what?'

'The questionnaire!'

'About what?' Uttering any more syllables than that would have been painful.

'The questionnaire on personnel, which I sent you a good two weeks ago! It was extremely urgent!'

'It was filled in and despatched.'

'To me?'

'Yes.'

'When?'

'Six days ago.' A whopping lie.

'Did you make a copy?'

'Yes.'

'If I can't find it, I'll let you know and you can send me the copy.'

'Okay.'

When he hung up, his shirt was dripping. 'Do you know anything about a questionnaire on personnel that the commissioner sent here about two weeks ago?' he asked Fazio.

'I remember giving it to you.'

'So where the hell did it end up? I have to find it and fill it in. He's liable to call back in half an hour. Let's look for it.'

'But the girl's still in your office.'

'I'll have to send her home.'

She was in the same position as she had been when they'd left her. She seemed not to have budged.

'Adriana, something's come up. Can we meet again this afternoon?'

'I'm supposed to be home by five, when the nurse leaves.'

'Shall we make it tomorrow morning?'

'That's the funeral.'

'Well, then, I don't know ...'

'I've got an idea. I invite you both to lunch. That way, we can continue talking. If you feel like it . . .'

'Thank you very much,' said Fazio, 'but I have to be at home. It's the fifteenth of August, after all.'

'I, on the other hand, would be delighted to come,' said Montalbano. 'Where will you take me?'

'Wherever you like.'

Montalbano couldn't believe it. They made an appointment to meet at Enzo's at one thirty.

'That girl's got balls of steel,' Fazio muttered, as she went out.

✼

Left alone, Montalbano and Fazio searched the room and became discouraged. The desk was covered with papers, and there were stacks on the filing tray with water and glasses, on top of the filing cabinet, and even on the little sofa and the two armchairs for important visitors.

They worked up a royal sweat and took a good half-hour to find the questionnaire. But the worst was yet to come, and they sweated even more while they were filling in the answers.

When they had finished it was past one o'clock. Fazio said goodbye and left.

'Catarella!'

'Here I am.'

'Photocopy these four pages for me. Then, if anyone from the commissioner's office should phone asking about a questionnaire, send them the copy you've made. But be absolutely certain: the copy!'

'Don' worry, Chief.'

'Now, get the clothes you hung out to dry and bring them to me. Then go and open my car doors.'

Undressing in the bathroom, he had the impression that he stank. It must have been all the effort he'd made searching for that damned questionnaire. He washed thoroughly, changed his clothes, gave Catarella the sweaty ones to put in the courtyard, and went into Augello's office. He knew that Mimì kept a little bottle of cologne in one of his drawers. He looked for it and found it. It was called Irresistible. He unscrewed the cap and, thinking that there was a dropper, managed to empty half the bottle over his shirt and trousers. Now what? Should he put the sweaty clothes back on? No, maybe out in the open air the cologne would evaporate. Then he had a moment of hesitation: should he bring the mini-fan? He decided against it. He would surely look ridiculous to Adriana, holding the little contraption to his face and smelling sweet as a whore.

Even though Catarella had opened the doors, the car was like a furnace. But he didn't feel up to walking all the way to Enzo's, especially as he was already late.

*

In front of the trattoria, which was closed, Adriana stood in the scorching sun, beside a Fiat Punto. He'd forgotten that Enzo celebrated the 15 August holiday by closing the restaurant. 'Follow me,' he said to the girl.

Near the bar in Marinella there was a trattoria he'd never tried. But, driving past in his car, he'd noticed that the tables outside were always in shade, protected by a very dense pergola. It took them ten minutes to get there. Despite the holiday, there weren't many people at the restaurant, and they were able to choose a table more isolated than the rest.

'Did you change and douse yourself with cologne for my sake?' Adriana asked mischievously.

'No, for my own. As for the cologne, the bottle spilled all over me,' he said gravely. He would probably have been better off smelling of sweat.

They sat in silence until the waiter appeared and recited the litany. 'An' we got spaghetti wit' tomata sauce, spaghetti in squid ink, spaghetti wit' sea urchin, spaghetti wit' clam sauce, spaghetti—'

'I'll have it with the clam sauce,' Montalbano interrupted him. 'And you?'

'With sea urchin.'

The waiter then began a different litany.

'For mains we got salt-baked mullet, baked gilthead, sea bass in sauce, grilled turbot—'

'You can tell us later,' said Montalbano.

The waiter looked offended. He returned a few minutes later with cutlery, glasses, water, and wine, white and ice-cold.

'Would you like some?'

'Yes.'

Montalbano poured her half a glass and the same for himself.

'It's good,' she said.

'Would you believe I can't remember where we left off?'

'You were asking me if Spitaleri and Rina had crossed paths on any other occasions, and I said yes.'

'Ah, yes, right. What did your sister say about that?'

'She said that after that time with Ralf, Spitaleri was hovering over her a bit too much.'

'In what sense?'

'Rina had the impression that he was spying on her. She would bump into him a little too regularly. For example, if she took the bus into town, on the way back Spitaleri would appear and offer her a lift home. And this, up until a week before.'

'A week before what?'

'Before the twelfth of October.'

'And Rina would let him drive her home?'

'Sometimes.'

'And did Spitaleri always behave?'

'Yes.'

'And what happened a week before your sister disappeared?'

'Something unpleasant. That evening, it was already dark, and Rina accepted the lift. But just after they turned on to the little road for Pizzo, in front of the house that belongs to that peasant who was later arrested, Spitaleri stopped the car and put his hands all over her. Just like that, out of the blue, according to Rina.'

'What did your sister do?'

'She screamed so loudly that the peasant came running outside. Rina saw her chance and took refuge in the man's house. Spitaleri was forced to leave.'

'How did Rina get home?'

'On foot. The peasant walked her back.'

'You said he was arrested?'

'Yes, poor thing. When police began looking for her, they searched his house as well. And, as luck would have it, they found one of my sister's earrings under a piece of furniture. Rina thought it had fallen off in Spitaleri's car, but in fact she'd lost it there. And I decided to tell the police what had happened with Spitaleri. But it was useless. You know how the police can be, don't you?'

'Yes, I do.'

'The poor man was persecuted for months.'

'Do you know if they questioned Spitaleri?'

'Of course. But Spitaleri told them that on the morning of the twelfth he'd left for Bangkok. It couldn't have been him.'

The waiter arrived with the spaghetti.

Adriana brought the first forkful to her mouth, tasted it, then said. 'It's good. Would you like to try some?'

'Why not?'

Montalbano reached over, armed with a fork, and wound some spaghetti on to it. The food wasn't comparable with Enzo's, but it was edible. 'You try mine.'

Adriana did as he had.

They didn't speak again until they had finished. Every now and then they looked at each other and smiled.

Something strange had occurred. It was as if the familiarity of sticking one's fork into the other's dish had established a sort of mutual confidence, an intimacy, that hadn't existed before.

FOURTEEN

They had finished eating for some time, but still weren't talking. As they each sipped a cold, digestive *limoncello*, Montalbano could feel her observing him, just as he had observed her at the station. Just to appear nonchalant – since it was hard to pretend nothing was happening, with those eyes the colour of the sea resting on him – he lit a cigarette.

'Could I have one, too, please?'

He held out the packet, she extracted a cigarette, put it between her lips, and half stood up, bending well forward for him to light it.

Don't forget she could be your daughter! the inspector admonished himself.

What he was seeing, thanks to the girl's position, made his head spin wildly. And the skin under his moustache was wet with sweat.

There was no way she didn't know that, by leaning forward in that manner, he was forced to look down her blouse. So why had she done it? To provoke him? But Adriana didn't seem the type to resort to such manipulation.

Or had she done it because she thought he had already reached an age where one no longer paid much attention to women? Yes, that must be it.

He didn't have time to feel sorry for himself before the girl, after she had taken two puffs, suddenly laid her hand on his.

Since Adriana showed no sign of feeling the heat – in fact, she looked as fresh as the proverbial daisy – the inspector was amazed to find she had such a burning touch. Was it the combination of their body heat, his and hers, that made the temperature increase? And, if not, just how hot was the blood circulating inside her?

'She was raped, wasn't she?'

It was the question that Montalbano, at every moment, had been expecting, fearing. He had prepared a good, articulate answer in advance, which he now completely forgot. 'No,' he said.

Why had he said that? So that he wouldn't have to see the light of beauty go out before him?

'You're not telling me the truth.'

'Believe me, Adriana, the post-mortem revealed that – '

' – she was a virgin?'

'Yes.'

'That's even worse,' she said.

'Why?'

'Because in that case the violence was even more horrific.'

The pressure from her hand, which now was scalding, increased.

'Could we drop the formalities?'

'If you like.'

'I want to tell you something in confidence.'

She let go of his hand, which suddenly felt cold, stood up, grabbed her chair, put it next to Montalbano's and sat down. Now she could speak softly, whisper. 'She most certainly was raped. I'm sure of it. When we were at the station I didn't want to tell you in front of that other man. But with you, it's different.'

'You mentioned that a few minutes before you had the pain in your throat you'd felt something else.'

'Yes. A sense of total, utter panic. A terror for my very existence. It had never happened to me before.'

'Try to explain it to me.'

'All of a sudden, as I was standing near the armoire, I saw my sister's image reflected in the mirror. She was upset, terrified. One second later I felt myself plunged into total darkness. Horrifying. It was as if I was enveloped in something slimy, without light or air, something malignant. A place — well, not really a place, but where every sort of horror or outrage became possible. Then, like what happens in nightmares, I tried to scream, but my voice made no sound. I also know I went blind for a few seconds, I groped around in the emptiness, then leaned against a wall so I wouldn't fall. And that was when—'

She stopped. Montalbano didn't say a word, didn't move. Sweat was dripping down his forehead.

'That was when I felt robbed.'

'How?' the inspector couldn't help but ask.

'Robbed of myself. It's hard to put into words. Someone was violently, ferociously taking possession of my body, separating it from me, to abuse it, humiliate it, annihilate it, to make it an object, a thing...' Her voice cracked.

'That's enough,' said Montalbano. And he took her hands in his.

'Is that what happened?' she asked.

'We think so.'

But why wasn't she crying? Her eyes had turned a darker blue, the lines at the corners of her mouth had deepened, but she wasn't crying.

What was it that gave her such strength, such inner toughness? Was it perhaps that she had known at the very moment she was killed Rina had died, while her mother and father had kept hoping their daughter was still alive?

And perhaps, over all these years, the pain, the sorrow, the tears had clotted into a kind of solid mass, a stony lump that would never again dissolve into an expression of pity for Rina or herself. 'A minute ago you said you saw your sister's image in the mirror. What did you mean?'

She smiled ever so slightly. 'It began as a game when we were five years old. We would stand in front of the mirror and talk. But not directly. We would each turn towards the other's reflection. We kept doing it, even as teenagers. When we had something really serious or secret to tell, we would go and stand in front of the mirror.'

The girl rested her head on Montalbano's shoulder for a moment. And he realized that it was not to seek comfort, but to alleviate the profound weariness she must have felt from speaking to a stranger about something so intimate, so secret.

Then she stood up decisively and looked at her watch. 'It's already three thirty. Shall we go?'

'If you want.'

But hadn't she said she could stay out until five?

Montalbano got up, feeling a little disappointed, and the waiter prepared the bill.

'Let me pay for this,' said Adriana, and she pulled some money out of the pocket of her jeans.

But when they were in the car park, she made no move towards her car. Montalbano gave her a puzzled look.

'Let's take yours,' she said.

'Where to?'

'If you've understood me, you've also understood where I want to go. I don't need to tell you.'

He had, of course, understood. He'd understood perfectly. But he was behaving like the soldier who doesn't want to go to war. 'Do you think it's appropriate?'

She didn't answer, just kept looking at him.

Montalbano realized that in the end he would not be able to say no to her. The soldier would go to war; there were no two ways about it. And, anyway, the sun was beating down on them like a sledgehammer in the car park. It was impossible to remain out in the open one moment longer.

'All right, get in.'

Getting into the car was like lying down on a grill. Montalbano regretted not bringing his mini-fan. Adriana opened all the windows. For the duration of the drive, she sat with her head leaning out the window, eyes closed.

The inspector, on the other hand, had a nagging question boring into his brain: wasn't he doing something incredibly stupid? Why had he agreed to go? Simply because the heat in the car park made it impossible to discuss things? But that was only an excuse. The truth was that he rather liked helping this girl, who—

Who could be your own daughter! his conscience interrupted.

You keep out of this! Montalbano replied angrily. *I was thinking of something entirely different, which is that this poor girl has been carrying a terrible weight inside her for six years, the exact intuition of what happened to her sister, and only now is she finding the strength to talk about it and unburden herself. It's only right to help her.*

You're a hypocrite, worse than Tommaseo, said the voice of his conscience.

As soon as they turned on to the track to Pizzo,

Adriana opened her eyes. When they were passing her house, she said, 'Stop!' She didn't get out, just looked at it from the car.

'We've never gone back since then. I know that from time to time Papa sends a woman to clean it and keep it in order, but we haven't had the courage to come here in the summer, like we used to do ... Okay, we can go now.'

When Montalbano pulled up in front of the last house, she was already opening the car door. 'Do you really have to do this, Adriana?'

'Yes.'

He left the car open, the keys in the ignition – there wasn't a living soul around.

Once out of the car, Adriana took his hand and brought it to her lips, resting them there for a moment, then continued holding it tightly. He led her to the side of the house where one could gain access to the illegal apartment. Forensics had placed two planks there to facilitate entry. The window to the small bathroom was covered with ribbons of coloured plastic of the sort that were used at roadworks. From one of these strips dangled a sheet of paper with stamps and signatures. It was the official seal. The inspector removed it all and went in first, telling the girl to wait for him. He turned on the torch he'd brought with him and checked all the rooms. The few minutes it took to walk round the apartment sufficed to drench him yet again in sweat. There was a sort of viscous humidity in those underground rooms, and it felt grimy, dirty; the heavy, stale air burned the eyes and throat.

He went back and helped the girl climb through the window.

Once inside, Adriana took the torch from him and headed straight for the living room.

As if she'd been there before, the inspector thought, bewildered, as he followed her.

She stopped in the doorway and shone the torch beam on the walls, the pile of frames wrapped in plastic, and the trunk. She appeared to have forgotten that Montalbano was beside her. She said nothing, but was breathing heavily...

'Adriana...'

The girl didn't hear him, only continued her personal descent into hell.

She started walking, but slowly, as though uncertain. She turned slightly to the left, towards the trunk, then to the right, took three steps and stopped.

As she was moving about in this manner Montalbano, who ended up almost in front of her, noticed her eyes were closed. She was looking for an exact spot, not with her eyes but with some other, unknown, sense that she alone must possess.

Having arrived to the left of the french windows, she placed her hands on the wall as though bracing herself, her legs spread apart.

'*Matre santa!*' Montalbano said in terror. Was he witnessing a sort of re-enactment of what had happened in that room? Was Adriana perhaps possessed by Rina's spirit?

All at once the torch fell to the floor. Luckily it didn't go out.

Adriana was standing in the exact spot that Forensics had placed the pool of blood. She was shaking all over.

It's not possible, it's not possible! Montalbano said to himself.

His rational mind refused to believe what he saw.

Then he heard a sound that paralysed him. Not weeping, but a kind of wail. Like that of a mortally wounded animal, long, sustained, soft. It was coming from Adriana.

Montalbano sprang, bent down, picked up the torch, grabbed the girl by the hips and pulled. But she resisted. It was as though her hands were glued to the wall. The inspector worked his way between her arms and the wall, shot the beam of the torch into her face, but the girl's eyes were still closed.

From her twisted, half-open mouth came the distressing wail, and now there was a thread of drool as well. Dismayed, he slapped her hard twice, with the front and the back of his hand.

Adriana opened her eyes, looked at him, then embraced him with all her might, pressing her body firmly against him and pushing him up against the wall. Then she kissed him hard, biting his lips. Montalbano felt the ground go from under his feet and clutched her as if to stop himself falling, as her kiss went on and on.

Then the girl let him go, ran to the bathroom window and climbed through it. Montalbano followed fast behind her, having no time to put the seals back up.

Adriana raced to his car, got into the driver's seat and turned on the ignition. Montalbano barely managed to get in on the other side before the car was pulling away.

Adriana stopped in front of her house, got out, ran to the door, searched in her pockets, found the key, opened the door and went in, leaving it open behind her.

By the time Montalbano was inside, she had gone.

What should he do now? He heard her vomiting somewhere.

He went outside and slowly walked round the house. The silence was total. Except for the thousands of cicadas, that was. At one time there must have been a field of wheat behind the house, because he saw a *pagliaro* there, a tall, narrow hut made of straw and wildflowers.

Under a clump of long-yellowed weeds, a sparrow was rolling around in the earth, cleaning itself in the absence of water.

He felt like doing the same. He, too, needed to clean himself – of the filth that had stuck to his skin when he was in the underground apartment.

Then, without realizing what he was doing, he did something he had done as a little boy. He took off his shirt, trousers and underwear and, naked, pressed his body against the *pagliaro*.

Then he opened his arms as wide as he could and embraced the hut, trying to stick his head as far inside as possible. He was forcing his way into the *pagliaro*, thrusting all of his bodyweight forwards, moving it first to the right, then to the left. And when, at last, he could smell the clean, dry odour of old straw, he breathed it in deep, and deeper still, until he detected a scent that surely existed only in his imagination, that of the sea breeze, which had managed to wend its way into the dense web of dried stalks and remain trapped therein. A sea breeze with a slightly bitter aftertaste, as if burned by the August heat.

All at once, half of the *pagliaro* collapsed on top of him, covering him.

He stayed there, immobile, feeling cleansed by every blade of straw that had come to rest on his skin.

Once, as a child, he had done the same thing, and his aunt, no longer seeing him anywhere, had started to call him. 'Salvo! Where are you? Salvo?'

But that wasn't his aunt's voice – Adriana was calling him, from just a few yards away!

He felt lost. He couldn't let her see him naked. What the hell had got into him? Why had he gone and done such a silly thing? Was he insane? Was the intense heat making him fuck up? How was he going to find a way out of this ridiculous situation?

'Salvo? Where are you? Sal—'

She must have spotted his clothes on the ground! He realized she was drawing closer.

She'd found him. *Matre santa*, how embarrassing! He closed his eyes, hoping to become invisible. He heard her laughing wildly, surely throwing back her beautiful head as she had done at the station. His heart was pounding with increased pressure. Now that was an idea: why couldn't he have a nice little heart attack? Then, more strongly than the scent of old straw, more strongly than the sea breeze, he smelled the overwhelming fragrance of her clean skin. She had had a shower. She must now be only inches away.

'If you stick out your arm, I'll hand you your things,' said Adriana.

Montalbano obeyed.

'All right, don't worry, I'm turning my back now,' she continued.

The only problem was that she kept laughing, humiliating him, the whole time he was clumsily getting dressed.

*

'I'm late,' Adriana said, as they were getting into the car. 'Would you let me drive?' She had realized that when it came to driving fast Montalbano was a lost cause.

For the entire journey – which was over quickly, with them pulling up in the restaurant's car park in the twinkling of an eye – she kept her right hand on his knee, driving with only her left. Was it her method of driving or the heat that had left the inspector bathed in sweat?

'Are you married?'

'No.'

'Do you have a girlfriend?'

'Yes, but she doesn't live in Vigàta.' Why had he blurted that out?

'What's her name?'

'Livia.'

'Where do you live?'

'In Marinella.'

'Give me your home phone number.'

Montalbano said it, and she repeated it.

'Already memorized.'

They arrived. The inspector got out of the car. She too. They found themselves standing in front of each other. Adriana put her hands on his hips and kissed him lightly. 'Thanks,' she said.

The inspector watched her drive away, tyres screeching.

＊

He decided not to drop in at the station but to go straight home. It was almost six o'clock when, in his swimming trunks, he opened the french windows giving on to the veranda. And there he found three youngsters sitting down, two boys and a girl, all about twenty. It was clear they had made his veranda their home for the entire day; they had eaten, drunk and taken off their clothes to go swimming there. Dozens of people were still on the beach, taking in the sun's last rays.

But scattered across the sand there were scraps of paper, leftovers, empty boxes and bottles. In short, it was a veritable dump. The veranda itself had been turned into a dump, the deck obscured with a hotch-potch of cigarette butts, roaches, cans of beer and Coca-Cola.

'Before you leave, I want you to clean all this up,' he said, descending the short flight of steps and heading towards the water.

'Okay, but you clean your arsehole first,' said one of the boys behind him.

The other two laughed.

He could have ignored it, but instead he turned and slowly approached them. 'Who said that?'

'Me,' said the huskier of the two in an arrogant tone.

'Come down here.'

He looked at his friends. 'Let's go and help the old man. I'll be back in a minute.'

The boy plonked himself in front of him, legs spread, then reached out and shoved him twice. 'Go and have your swim, Grandpa.'

Montalbano started him off with a left, which he dodged, while his right, just as planned, got him square in the face and dropped him to the ground, half unconscious.

It wasn't so much a punch as a wallop. The other two quickly stopped laughing. 'When I get back, I want it all cleaned up.'

He had to swim out quite a way to find clear water: closer to shore all manner of foreign objects, from turds to plastic cups, were floating on the surface. A pigsty.

Before going back, he looked shorewards, searching for a spot where there were fewer people and therefore the water was probably less filthy. This meant, however, that he had to walk for half an hour along the beach to get back to his house.

The kids were gone. And the veranda was clean.

In the shower, which was still warm, he thought of the punch that had almost knocked the kid out. How could he possibly be still capable of such strength? Then he realized it hadn't been down only to strength, but to the violent release of the tension that had built up inside him on that 15 August.

FIFTEEN

Late that evening, the families with little kids crying one minute and screaming the next, the drunken, brawling parties of friends, the young couples stuck so tightly together you couldn't have separated them with a knife, the solitary males with mobile phones glued to their ears, the other young couples with radios, CD players and other noise-making gadgets finally vacated the beach.

They went away, but their rubbish remained.

Rubbish, the inspector thought, had become the unmistakable sign that man had passed through any given place. In fact, they said Mount Everest had become a dump, and even outer space. Ten thousand years from now, the sole proof that man had once lived on the earth would be the discovery of enormous car cemeteries, the only surviving monument of a former, ahem, civilization.

After he'd been sitting awhile on the veranda, he noticed that the air stank. The rubbish covering the beach was no longer visible in the darkness, yet the stench of swift putrefaction in the extreme heat still wafted up to his nostrils.

There was no point in remaining outside. But neither was it possible to stay in with all the windows closed to keep out the stink, because the heat that the walls had absorbed during the day would never have a chance to dispel.

He got dressed, took the car and headed for Pizzo. Arriving at the house, he pulled up, got out and made for the staircase that led down to the beach.

He sat on the first step and lit a cigarette. He'd been right. The spot was too high up to be affected by the smell of rot from the rubbish that must surely lie across that beach, too.

He tried not to think of Adriana, but didn't succeed.

He stayed there for two hours, and by the time he got up to go home, he had come to the conclusion that the less he saw of the girl, the better.

*

'So, what did Miss Adriana tell you yesterday?' Fazio asked.

'Something I hadn't known for certain but had imagined. Do you remember when Dipasquale told us, and Adriana confirmed, that Rina had been assaulted by Ralf and that Spitaleri had saved her?'

'Of course.'

The inspector then recounted the whole story of how

from that moment on Spitaleri had been constantly after Rina until finally he had groped her in his car, and the girl was saved when a peasant appeared on the scene. And he also mentioned how the peasant had been made to run the gauntlet by police when one of Adriana's earrings was found in his house even though the poor man had had nothing to do with the crime.

He said not a word about the fact that he had gone back to the house in Pizzo with Adriana or about what had happened there.

'In conclusion,' said Fazio, 'we've got nothing to work with. It can't have been Ralf, because he was impotent, it can't have been Spitaleri because he was gone, and it can't have been Dipasquale because he's got an alibi.'

'Dipasquale's position is the weakest,' said the inspector. 'His alibi may have been made up.'

'Yes, but try to prove that.'

*

'Chief, iss Porxecutor Dommaseo.'

'Put 'im on.'

'Montalbano? I've made a decision.'

'Tell me.'

'I'm going to do it.'

And he was telling *him* about it? 'You're going to do what?'

'Hold a press conference.'

'But what need is there for that?'

'Oh, there's need, Montalbano, there's need.'

The only need was Tommaseo's to appear on television.

'The newsmen,' the prosecutor continued, 'have got wind of something and are asking questions. I don't want to run the risk of them giving a distorted image of the overall picture.'

What overall picture? 'It's true that's a pretty big risk.'

'So you agree?'

'Have you already set it up?'

'Yes, for tomorrow morning at eleven. Will you be there?'

'No. And what will you say?'

'I'll talk about the crime.'

'Will you say she was raped?'

'Well, I'll suggest it.'

Great! It took less than a suggestion to have the journalists jump all over that sort of subject! 'And what if they ask if you have any idea as to the murderer?'

'Well, one has to be adroit in these situations.'

'As you are.'

'In all modesty ... I'll say that we're following two leads: the first is that we're checking the masons' alibis, and the second is that we're investigating a maniac drifter who forced the girl to go with him into the underground apartment. Are you in agreement?'

'Perfectly.' A maniac drifter! And how would a maniac

drifter have known about the secret illegal apartment if the construction site was fenced off?

'For today, I've called Adriana back in for questioning,' Tommaseo said. 'I want to break down any residual defences she may have, to interrogate her thoroughly — thoroughly and at great length — and lay her completely bare.'

His voice had turned shrill. Montalbano was afraid that with two more words the guy would start moaning and saying, *Ah, ah, ah*, like in a porn flick.

*

It was already becoming a habit. Before going to Enzo's trattoria, he changed his clothes and gave the sweaty ones to Catarella. Then, after eating — though he ate sparingly, having little appetite — he felt listless and decided to go home to Marinella.

Miracle of miracles! Four dustmen had nearly finished cleaning the beach! He put on his trunks and dived into the sea in search of relief from the heat. Afterwards he dozed for an hour.

*

By four o'clock he was back at the station. But he didn't feel like doing anything.

'Catarella!'

'Whattaya need, Chief?'

'Don't let anyone into my office without alerting me first. Is that clear?'

'Yessir.'

'Oh, and did anyone call from Montelusa about the questionnaire?'

'Yessir, Chief, I sennit over to 'em.'

He locked the door to his room, stripped down to his underpants, threw the papers that were on the armchair on to the floor, pulled this up next to the mini-fan, which he turned in such a way that it blew onto his chest, then sat down, hoping to survive.

*

An hour later the telephone rang. 'Chief, iss a marshal called La Caña says 'e's wit' da Finance Police.'

'Put him on.'

'I can't put 'im on, seeing as how the beforementioned marshal is 'ere poissonally in poisson.'

God, and he was practically naked!

'Tell him I'm on the phone, wait five minutes, then let him in.'

He got dressed in a hurry. His clothes were exactly the same as when he'd just stretched them out to dry, still saturated with heat. He opened the door and went out to meet Laganà, brought him into the office, sat him down, and locked the door. He felt embarrassed to find the marshal dressed in a suit that looked as if he'd just picked it up from the cleaners.

'Would you like anything to drink, Marshal?'

'No, thanks, Inspector. Whatever I drink only makes me sweat.'

'Why did you put yourself out? You could have phoned...'

'Inspector, nowadays it's better not to say certain things over the phone.'

'Maybe we ought to use little folded-up pieces of paper, like Provenzano.'

'They'd probably be intercepted, too. The only way is to talk in person and, if possible, in a safe place.'

'I think it's safe here.'

'Let's hope so.'

The marshal slipped a hand into his jacket pocket, extracted a sheet of paper folded in four and handed it to Montalbano. 'Is this what you were interested in?'

It was the receipt from Ribaudo Enterprises for some innocent pipes and some safety railings, delivered on 27 July to the Spitaleri construction site in Montelusa. It was signed by Filiberto Attanasio, the watchman. Montalbano felt heartened. 'Thank you, this is exactly what I was looking for. Did anyone notice?'

'I don't think so. This morning we seized two crates of documents. As soon as I found that receipt, I had it photocopied and brought it here to you.'

'I don't know how to thank you.'

Marshal Laganà stood up. So did Montalbano.

'I'll see you out.'

As they were shaking hands in the main entrance to the station, Laganà said, with a smile, 'There's no point in my insisting that you say nothing to anyone about how that document was obtained.'

'Marshal, you're offending me.'

Laganà hesitated a moment, turned serious, then said in a low voice, 'Be careful how you deal with Spitaleri.'

*

'Federico? Montalbano here.'

Inspector Lozupone seemed truly happy to hear from him. 'Salvo! What a pleasant surprise! How are you?'

'Fine. And you?'

'Fine, thanks. Do you need anything?'

'I'd like to talk to you.'

'Of course. Fire away.'

'In person.'

'Is it urgent?'

'Fairly.'

'Look, I'll definitely be in my office until—'

'Better outside somewhere.'

'Ah. We could meet at the Caffe Marino at—'

'Not in public.'

'You're frightening me, Salvo. Where, then?'

'Either at my place or yours.'

'I have a curious wife.'

'Then come to my house in Marinella. You know where it is. Ten o'clock tonight okay with you?'

*

At eight, as the inspector was leaving the office, Tommaseo called. He sounded disappointed. 'I want confirmation from you.'

'I confirm.'

'Excuse me, Montalbano, but what are you confirming?'

'Ah, well, I don't know what, but if you're asking me for confirmation, I'm ready to give it.'

'Even if you don't know what you're supposed to confirm?'

'I see. You don't want generic confirmation but specific.'

'I'd say so!'

Every now and then he liked to mess with Tommaseo's head. 'Then tell me what it is.'

'That girl, Adriana, today ... Among other things, she was even more beautiful. I don't know how she does it. She's like the essence of woman. Whatever she says, whatever she does, one is left utterly charmed and ... Ah, never mind, what was I saying?'

'That one is left utterly charmed.'

'My God, no, I was just saying that incidentally. Ah, yes. Adriana told me her sister had been assaulted, luckily without consequences, by a young German who later died in a railway disaster in Germany. I'm going to mention this at the press conference.'

Railway disaster? What the hell had Tommaseo understood?

'But no matter how much pressure I put on her,' the prosecutor continued, 'she couldn't or wouldn't tell me any more, claiming it was pointless for me to continue interrogating her, since she and her twin sister never confided in each other and, she added, often quarrelled so violently that their parents did all they could to keep them apart. In fact, the day Rina was murdered, Adriana wasn't even in Vigàta. So, since the girl told me you questioned her yesterday, my question to you is, did she also tell you she didn't get on with her sister?'

'Absolutely! She said they even came to blows two or three times a day.'

'So it's useless to call her in for further questioning?'

'I'm afraid so.'

Obviously Adriana had grown sick and tired of Tommaseo and made up that lie, knowing she could count on the inspector's complicity.

*

Adriana phoned him at home around nine that evening. 'Can I drop round in about an hour?'

'I'm sorry, but I have an engagement.' And if he hadn't, what would he have answered?

'What a shame. I wanted to take advantage of the fact that my aunt and uncle are here from Milan. I told you about them. They were the ones who lived in Montelusa.'

'I remember.'

'They came for the funeral.'

He'd completely forgotten about it. 'When is it?'

'Tomorrow morning. They're leaving immediately afterwards. Don't make any engagements for tomorrow evening. I'm hoping my nurse friend can come.'

'Adriana, I have a job that—'

'Try to do your best. Oh, Tommaseo called me in for questioning today. He was positively drooling as he stared at my tits. And to think that I'd put on a reinforced bra for the occasion. I told him a lie to get him out of my hair once and for all.'

'I know what you said to him. He phoned me to ask if it was true that you and Rina couldn't stand one another.'

'What did you say?'

'I confirmed it.'

'I knew I could count on you. I love you. See you tomorrow.'

He ran into the bathroom and got into the shower before Lozupone arrived. Those three words, *I love you*, had immediately made him break out in a drenching sweat.

*

Lozupone was five years his junior, a man of powerful build and pithy speech. Not the sort to set tongues wagging, he was honest and had always done his duty. Montalbano, therefore, had to proceed carefully with him and choose the right words. He offered him a whisky and sat him down on the veranda. Luckily a light wind was blowing.

'Salvo, get to the point. What do you have to tell me?'

'It's a delicate matter, and before I make any moves, I want to talk to you about it.'

'Here I am.'

'I've been working on the murder of a girl . . .'

'Yes, I've heard about it.'

'And I happened to interrogate a builder named Spitaleri, whom you also know.'

Lozupone seemed to react defensively. 'What do you mean, I know him? I only know him because I investigated the accidental death of a mason at one of his construction sites in Montelusa.'

'That's just it. I wanted to know more about this investigation of yours. What conclusion did you come to?'

'I think I told you a second ago: accidental death. The work site, when I went there, was up to scratch. I allowed it to reopen after it had been closed for five days. Laurentano, the prosecutor, was pressing me to hurry up.'

'When were you first called?'

'On the Monday morning after the mason's body was found. And I repeat, all the safety measures were in order. The only possible conclusion was that the Arab, who'd had a bit too much to drink, climbed over the protective railing and fell. And, in fact, the post-mortem showed that there was more wine than blood in his body.'

Montalbano baulked, but didn't let Lozupone see it. If things had really happened the way Lozupone said and Spitaleri maintained, why had Filiberto told a different story? Most importantly, didn't the receipt from Ribaudo's prove that the watchman had been telling the truth? Wasn't it better to play straight with Lozupone and tell him what he, Montalbano, thought about the matter?

'Federì, didn't it occur to you that maybe, when the mason fell, there wasn't any protection and that the railing was put up on Sunday? So that when you came on Monday morning everything would be in order?'

Lozupone refilled his glass with whisky. 'Of course it occurred to me,' he said.

'And what did you do?'

'What you yourself would have done.'

'Namely?'

'I asked Spitaleri which firm had supplied his scaffolding. He said Ribaudo's so I reported this to Laurentano. I wanted him to question Ribaudo, or to authorize me to question Ribaudo, but he said no. He said that, for him, the investigation ended there.'

'The proof you were looking for from Ribaudo I managed to procure. Spitaleri had the materials sent that Sunday at dawn, and he assembled it with the help of the work foreman Dipasquale and the watchman Attanasio.'

'And what do you intend to do with this proof?'

'Give it either to you or to Prosecutor Laurentano.'

'Let me see it.'

Montalbano handed him the receipt. Lozupone looked at it and handed it back. 'This doesn't prove anything.'

'Didn't you see the date? The twenty-seventh of July was a Sunday!'

'You know what Laurentano might say to you? First, that given the working relationship between Spitaleri and Ribaudo, it wasn't the first time that Ribaudo had furnished materials to Spitaleri on a Sunday. Second, that the material was needed because on Monday morning they were supposed to begin construction on several new floors of the building. Third, would you please explain to me, Inspector Montalbano, how you happened to get your hands on this document? To conclude, Spitaleri gets away with it while you and whoever gave you the document are screwed.'

'But is Laurentano in on this?'

'Laurentano? What are you saying? Laurentano only wants to advance his career. And if you're going to get ahead, rule number one is to let sleeping dogs lie.'

Montalbano felt so enraged that he blurted out, 'And what does your father-in-law, Lattes, think about it?'

'Lattes? Don't stray too far, Salvo. Don't piss into the wind. My father-in-law has certain political interests, it's true, but he's certainly never said anything to me about this Spitaleri business.'

And why do you think that is? Montalbano felt satisfied with this answer. 'So you give up?'

'What else, in your opinion, should I do? Start tilting at windmills like Don Quixote?'

'Spitaleri is not a windmill.'

'Montalbà, let's be frank. Do you know why Laurentano won't let me take it any further? Because when he puts Spitaleri and his political protectors on one side of his personal scale and the dead body of an anonymous Arab immigrant on the other, which way do you think that scale tips? The death of the Arab was given three lines of coverage in only one newspaper. What do you think will happen if we go after Spitaleri? A pandemonium of television, radio, newspapers, questions in Parliament, pressure, maybe even blackmail. And so I ask you, how many people, among us and among the judges, have the same scale in their offices as Laurentano?'

SIXTEEN

He felt so furious that he stayed out on the veranda to finish the bottle of whisky, specifically intending, if not to get drunk, then at least to numb himself enough to be able to go to bed.

After thinking it over, with a cool head and without getting too carried away, he realized Lozupone was right. He would never succeed in nailing Spitaleri with the evidence that had seemed so important to him.

And then supposing Laurentano did find the courage to take action and some heedless colleague of his managed to bring the case to trial, any lawyer could pick apart that evidence in the twinkling of an eye. But was it really because the evidence was negligible – since it still was evidence, after all – that Spitaleri would not be found guilty? Or was it because in today's Italy, thanks to laws that increasingly favoured the rights of the accused, what was lacking above all was a firm resolve to send anyone who had committed a crime to prison?

But why, on the other hand, had the inspector had from the start, and continued to have, such a strong desire to harm the developer? Because he was guilty of a building violation? Come on! If that was the case, he should have something against half the population of Sicily, since illegal constructions almost outnumbered the legal ones.

Why had somebody died at one of his work sites?

And how many so-called accidents in the workplace took place that weren't accidents at all but genuine murders by the employers?

No, there was another reason.

Fazio's report that Spitaleri liked underage girls, and his own conclusion that the builder was a sex tourist, had made him develop a violent aversion to the man. He couldn't stand the kind of people who took aeroplanes from one continent to another to exploit poverty, and material or moral misery in the most ignoble manner possible.

Someone like that, even if he lived in a palace in his home country, travelled first class, stayed in ten-star hotels and ate in restaurants where a fried egg cost a hundred thousand euros, was a wretch deep in his soul, more wretched than the bastard who robbed churches of their alms boxes or children of their lunch boxes for the sheer pleasure of doing so rather than because he was starving.

And men of that ilk are surely capable of the vilest, most loathsome acts.

At last, after some two hours, his eyelids were drooping. There was one finger of whisky left in the glass. He knocked it back and it went down the wrong way. As he was coughing, he remembered something Lozupone had said.

Which was that the post-mortem had confirmed that the Arab had drunk too much, and had fallen for that reason.

But there was another hypothesis.

That the Arab, when he fell, had not died. He had been only mortally injured, and therefore able to swallow. And Spitaleri, Dipasquale and Filiberto had taken advantage of the situation and forcibly plied him with wine, then left him to die.

They were capable of such an act, and the idea must have come to the one most capable of all: Spitaleri. And if things had happened as he was imagining, it wasn't just he, Inspector Montalbano, who was being thwarted, but justice itself – indeed the very notion of justice.

*

He didn't sleep a wink all night. His rage combined with the heat to make him sweat so much that around four o'clock in the morning he got up and changed the sheets. For nothing: half an hour later they were as drenched as the ones he had discarded.

By eight o'clock he could no longer bear to stay in

bed. Restlessness, nerves and the heat were driving him crazy.

It occurred to him that Livia, on a boat out on the open sea, must be having a better time of it than him so he tried ringing her on her mobile phone. A recorded woman's voice informed him that the phone of the person he'd called was switched off and that, if he wished, he could call back later.

Naturally, at that hour, the young lady was either asleep or too busy helping her dear cousin Massimiliano to manoeuvre the boat. Suddenly he was itching all over and scratching himself almost raw.

He hopped down from the veranda on to the beach. The sand was already hot and burned the soles of his feet. He went for a long swim. Far from the shore the water was still cool, but his refreshment didn't last long. He was dry by the time he got back to the house.

Why bother to go to the station? he asked himself. He didn't have anything pressing to do; in fact, he had nothing to do. Tommaseo was busy with his press conference; Adriana had her sister's funeral to attend; the commissioner was probably too busy to look at the answers on the questionnaire he had sent to the different police forces. And he, Montalbano, felt only like lolling about, but not at home.

'Catarella?'

'Atcher soivice, Chief.'

'Lemme talk to Fazio.'

'Straight aways.'

'Fazio? I'm not coming in this morning.'

'Are you ill?'

'I'm fine. But I'm convinced that I'll feel terrible if I come in to work.'

'You're right, Chief. It's stifling here. Nobody can breathe.'

'I'll be there this evening around six.'

'Okay. Oh, Chief, can I borrow your mini-fan?'

'Don't break it.'

*

Half an hour later, on the road to Pizzo, he stopped in front of the rustic cottage, the one the peasant lived in. He got out of the car and approached the house. The front door was open. 'Anyone in?' he called.

At the window directly above the door appeared the same man whose earthenware pot Gallo had shattered with the car. From the way he looked at him, the inspector could see he didn't recognize him.

'What d'you want?'

If he told him he was with the police, the man might not let him in. The homely clucking of some chickens behind the house came to his aid. He took a wild guess. 'Have you any fresh eggs?'

'How many do you need?'

It couldn't be a big chicken coop. 'Half a dozen should do.'

'Come in.'

Montalbano entered.

A bare room that must have served the man's every purpose. A table, two chairs, a cupboard. Against one wall, a small stove with a gas cylinder, and beside it a marble surface with glasses, dishes, a frying-pan and a pot on top. Humble utensils worn with time and overuse. A hunting rifle hung on one wall.

The peasant came down the wooden stairs leading to the room above, which must have been his bedroom. 'I'll go and fetch them for you.'

He went outside. The inspector sat down in a chair.

The man returned with three eggs in each hand. He took two steps towards the small table, then stopped short. He stared hard at Montalbano as his face paled.

'What's wrong?' the inspector asked, getting up.

'Aaaaah!' the peasant roared. And with all his might he hurled the three eggs in his right hand at Montalbano's head. Although he was caught by surprise, the inspector dodged two, but the third hit his left shoulder and broke, dripping onto his shirt.

'Now I recognize you – you're a cop!'

'But listen—'

'Still the same story? Eh?'

'No, I came to—'

Of the other three eggs, one got him on the forehead and two in the chest. Montalbano was blinded. He brought his handkerchief to his eyes to wipe them, and when he was able to see again the peasant was holding the hunting rifle and pointing it straight at him. 'Get out of my house!'

The inspector ran. His colleagues must have put the poor man through a lot.

The stains had spread so far over his shirt that it was one colour at the front and another at the back.

He returned to Marinella to change his clothes. There he found Adelina scrubbing the floor. 'Signò, what happened? Somebuddy trow eggs at you?'

'Yes, poor bastard. I'm going to change.'

He washed himself in the hot water from the tanks on his roof, then put on a clean shirt. 'See you later, Adelì.'

'Signore, I cannotta come tomorra.'

'Why not?'

'Cause I'ma going to go see my boy, the bigger one, who's in jail in Montelusa.'

'How's the younger one doing?'

''E's in jail too, but in Palermo.'

She had two sons, both delinquents, who were always in and out of jail.

Montalbano himself had sent them there a couple of times, but he still remained fond of them. He was even godfather to one. 'Tell him I said hi.'

'I will. Since I'ma not coming, I make-a you somethin'
a eat.'

'Just cold things, though. That way they'll last longer.'

He headed back to Pizzo, with his swimming trunks
this time.

*

He sped past the peasant's cottage, worried that the man
might shoot at his car, then past Adriana's, whose doors
and windows were shuttered, and pulled up at the illegal
house.

Since he had the keys, he went inside, undressed, put
on his trunks, went back outside and down the stone
staircase to the beach. At this point there were few
swimmers, most of whom were speaking foreign languages.
After 15 August, Sicilians considered the summer season
over, even if the heat was worse than before.

He retained a memory of clean, refreshing pleasure
from the first time he had swum in those waters, when he
had come here with Callara. He dived into the sea and
stayed there until the skin on his fingertips wrinkled, a
sign that it was time to return to shore.

He intended to have a cold shower and go home to
eat whatever gift of God Adelina had prepared for him,
but the climb up the staircase with the hot sun high
overhead drained him. In the house, he went straight to
the master bedroom and lay down on the double bed.

It was two thirty when he fell asleep and almost five when he woke up. The mattress bore the imprint of his naked body, a damp silhouette.

He stayed in the shower so long that he used all the water in the tank. But since he wasn't at home, and as the house wasn't inhabited, he didn't regret it.

When he went out to go to the station, another car was parked in front of the house. He thought he'd seen it before, but he couldn't remember where. No one was around. Maybe they'd gone down to the beach.

Then he noticed that an electrical cable had been plugged into the socket next to the door and ran round the corner of the house to the back. Surely it was to illuminate the illegal apartment downstairs.

Who could it be? Certainly not Forensics. He was sure it must be some journalist who had come on the sly to take photos of the 'site of the atrocious crime', and was suddenly overcome with fury. How dared the brute?

He ran to his car, took his pistol out of the glove compartment and slipped it inside his belt. Past the corner, the electrical cable continued along the wall, ran over the planks and disappeared inside the window that served as an entrance to the illegal apartment. He climbed lightly over the ledge and found himself in the bathroom. Craning his neck cautiously, he saw that the living room was illuminated.

That fucking photographer was surely hoping to get a

scoop by taking pictures of the trunk in which the body had been found.

I'll give you a scoop, idiot, the inspector thought.

Then he did two things at once. First, he ran towards the living room, yelling, 'Hands up!' Second, he cocked his revolver and fired one shot into the air.

Now, either because the rooms were empty of furniture and therefore amplified noise, or because the apartment was entirely covered with plastic, which didn't allow sound to disperse, the shot sounded like a huge explosion, barely less than a bomb blast. The first person to take fright was Montalbano himself, who had the impression that the gun had exploded in his hand. Deafened he burst into the living room.

In terror, the photographer had dropped his camera and, trembling all over, was kneeling down with his hands raised and his forehead on the ground. He looked like an Arab praying.

'You are under arrest!' the inspector said. 'Montalbano's the name!'

'Wha – wha—' the man whimpered, barely raising his head.

'You want to know why? Because you broke the seals to come inside!'

'But – but – there weren't—'

'There weren't any seals!' said a quaking voice, coming from it wasn't clear where.

Montalbano looked about but couldn't see anyone. 'Who said that?'

'I did.'

And from behind the plastic-wrapped stack of window frames Callara's head popped out. 'Inspector, you have to believe us! There weren't any seals!'

At that moment Montalbano remembered that when he had been chasing Adriana he hadn't had time to put them back. 'Some young hooligan must have taken them down,' he said.

In the living room the flood-lamp made the air even hotter than it would normally have been. He could barely speak – his throat was parched. 'Let's get out of here,' he said.

They followed him into the apartment above, drank big glasses of mineral water, then sat in the living room with the french windows wide open.

'I was so scared I nearly had a heart attack,' said the man Montalbano had mistaken for a photographer.

'Me too,' said Callara. 'Every time I set foot in this damned house something strange happens!'

'My name's Paladino,' the man with the camera introduced himself. 'I'm a builder.'

'But what were you two doing here?'

Callara spoke first. 'Inspector, since there's not much time left to make the amnesty request, and since Mrs Gudrun's papers arrived by courier this morning, I pleaded with Mr Paladino to start doing the things that need to be done—'

'And the first thing that absolutely needs to be done is to document and photograph the illegal construction,' Paladino cut in. 'The photos will then be attached to the blueprints.'

'Did you finish taking your photographs?'

'I need another three or four of the living room.'

'Let's go.'

He went out with them, accompanied them as far as the window but did not go inside. Instead he stopped to collect the tape that had ended up under the two planks and set it aside. 'I'll wait for you upstairs.'

He smoked two cigarettes sitting at one end of the low wall along the terrace, in a spot where the sun wasn't beating down.

Then Callara came out. 'We've finished.'

'Where's Paladino?'

'Putting his equipment in the car. He'll be back in a second to say goodbye.'

'If you need to come again, let me know first.'

'Thanks. By the way, I must ask you something, Inspector.'

'What?'

'When will the seals come down?'

'Are you in a hurry?'

'Well, sort of. I'd like to set a date with Spitaleri for

digging the place out and restoring it. If I don't book ahead, that man, with all the things he's got going on—'

'If Spitaleri can't do it, find someone else.'

Paladino came back. 'We can go now.'

'I can't,' Callara said.

'What do you mean, you can't?'

'There's a written guarantee I didn't know about. I found it among the papers that arrived this morning from Germany.'

'Help me to understand this a little better.'

'It's a standard agreement,' said Paladino. 'Callara showed it to me.'

'What does it entail?'

This time it was Callara who spoke. 'It says that Angelo Speciale promises to employ the firm of Michele Spitaleri to dig out and restore the outside and inside walls of the illegal apartment once amnesty is granted. And he also promises not to turn to any other firms in the event that Spitaleri is busy with other jobs at the time, but to wait until he is available.'

'A simple contract,' said Montalbano.

'Yes, but properly executed, signed and countersigned. And if one of the parties fails to uphold it, especially with a character like Spitaleri, they may have serious problems on their hands,' said Paladino.

'Excuse me, Mr Paladino, but have you come across this sort of thing before?'

'This is the first time. I've never seen an agreement

like this made so far in advance. And I don't understand it. I ask myself, what's a twopenny-ha'penny job like this to someone like Spitaleri?'

'I'm sure,' said Callara, 'it was Speciale who wanted this agreement. He knew he could count on Spitaleri, and there would be no need for him to be around when the work got under way.'

'Did you see the date?'

'Yes, the twenty-seventh of October 1999, the day before Angelo Speciale left to go back to Germany.'

'Mr Callara, I'll have the seals removed as soon as possible.'

*

In the meantime, he put them back up. Then he got into his car and left. But he stopped after he'd driven just a few yards.

The front door and two windows of Adriana's house were open. Had the girl gone there in search of a little peace after the gloom of the funeral?

The inspector felt torn. Should he pop in to see her or continue on his way?

Then he saw an elderly woman, a housekeeper, no doubt, close the two windows, one after the other. He waited a little longer. The woman came out of the front door, then locked it.

Montalbano put the car into gear and drove to the station, a little disappointed yet a little relieved.

SEVENTEEN

'This morning I went to the funeral,' said Fazio.

'Were there many people?'

'Indeed there were, Inspector, all overcome with emotion, of course. Women fainting, crying, former schoolfriends with pale faces – the usual drama, in short. And when the coffin left the church, everyone clapped. Can you tell me why anyone would clap for the dead?'

'Perhaps because they thought she did the right thing by dying.'

'Are you joking, Chief?'

'No. When do people clap? When they've seen something they like. Logically, then, it should mean, "I'm rather pleased you're no longer in my hair." Who of the family was there?'

'The father. He was being held up by a man and woman who must have been relatives. Miss Adriana wasn't there. She must have stayed at home with her mother.'

'I have to tell you something you're not going to like.'

And he told him about his meeting with Lozupone. When he had finished, Fazio showed no surprise.

'You've nothing to say?'

'What am I supposed to say, Chief? I was expecting it. By hook or by crook, Spitaleri's going to weasel his way out, now and for ever, *in saecula saeculorum.*'

'Amen. Speaking of Spitaleri, I want you to do me a favour and give him a call. I have no desire to speak to him.'

'What do you want me to ask him?'

'If, when he left for Bangkok on the twelfth of October, he remembers what day he came back.'

'I'll do it now.'

He returned about ten minutes later.

'I tried his mobile phone, but it was switched off. So I rang his office, but he wasn't in. The secretary, however, looked it up in an old diary and said Spitaleri definitely returned on the afternoon of the twenty-sixth. She told me she remembered the day well.'

'Did she say why?'

'Chief, that lady's such a chatterbox that, if you don't stop her, she's liable to talk all day. She said the twenty-sixth of October is her birthday, and she was thinking Spitaleri wouldn't remember, but he gave her not only the orchid Thai Airways presents to every passenger but a box of chocolates. And there you have it. Why did you want to know?'

'Well, today I went to Pizzo for a dip. As I was about

to leave...' And he told him the whole story. 'Which means,' he concluded, 'that the following day he drew up this contract, perhaps because he'd found out that Angelo Speciale was about to leave for Germany.'

'I don't see anything odd about it,' said Fazio. 'And I'm sure it was Speciale himself who asked for the contract, as Callara said. By that point he trusted Spitaleri.'

Montalbano seemed unconvinced. 'Something doesn't make sense.'

The telephone rang. It was Catarella, terrified. 'Jesus-JesusJesus! Iss the c'mishner onna line!'

'So?'

'He sounds crazy, Chief! Wit' all doo respeck, he sounds like a rapid dog!'

'Put him on and have a nip of cognac. It'll calm your nerves.'

He turned on the speaker and gestured to Fazio to listen in. 'Good evening, Commissioner.'

'Good evening, my arse!'

As far as he could remember, Montalbano had never heard Commissioner Bonetti-Alderighi use an obscenity. Whatever the problem was, it must be a big one. 'Commissioner, I don't understand why—'

'The questionnaire!'

Montalbano felt relieved. Was that all? He gave a little smile. 'But, Commissioner, the questionnaire in question is no longer in question.' What fun it was to apply every now and then the teachings of the great master Catarella!

'What are you saying?'

'I've already dealt with it and sent it over to you.'

'Oh, you dealt with it, all right! You really did!'

So why was he ranting on about it? What was the problem? He asked the question: 'So, what's the problem?'

'Montalbano, are you working overtime at getting on my nerves today?'

That 'working overtime' made the inspector stop joking and counterattack. 'What are you saying? You're raving, sir!'

The commissioner appeared to calm down. 'Listen, Montalbano, I have the patience of Job, but if you're trying to make a fool of me . . .'

Ah, 'the patience of Job', too! Was the man trying to drive him out of his mind? 'Just tell me what I've done and stop threatening me.'

'What you've done? You sent me last year's questionnaire! Did you hear me? Last year's questionnaire!'

'How time flies!'

The commissioner was so beside himself that he didn't hear what the inspector had said. 'I'm giving you two hours, Montalbano. I want you to find the new questionnaire, answer the questions and fax it to me within two hours. Do you understand? Two hours!' He hung up.

Montalbano looked disconsolately at the ocean of

papers he had to wade through again. 'Fazio, will you do me a favour?'

'At your service, Chief.'

'Would you shoot me, please?'

＊

It took them three hours in all: two to find the questionnaire, one to fill it in. At a certain point they realized that it was exactly the same as the one from the previous year, with the same questions, in the same order; only the date in the heading had changed. They made no comment. They no longer had the strength to say what they thought about bureaucracy.

'Catarella!'

'Here I am.'

'Send this fax to the c'mishner right away and tell him to stick it you know where.'

Catarella turned pale. 'I can't, Chief.'

'That's an order, Cat!'

'Well, Chief, if you say it's an order . . .'

Resigned, he turned to leave. But wait! Catarella was only too liable to do it!

'No! Just send him the fax. Don't say anything.'

＊

How many tons of dust can there be among the papers in an office? At home, Montalbano spent a good half-hour

in the shower, then put on fresh clothes; the others stank
of sweat.

He was heading towards the refrigerator in his underpants to see what Adelina had prepared for him when the
telephone rang.

It was Adriana. She didn't say hi, didn't ask how he
was, but shot straight to the point. 'I can't make it to your
place tonight. My nurse friend isn't free. She'll be coming
here tomorrow morning. But you're working then, aren't
you?'

'Yes.'

'I want to see you.'

Quiet, Montalbano, quiet. Bite your tongue, Salvo.
Don't say, 'Me too,' as you were about to.

The girl's words, practically whispered, had made him
break into a sweat.

'I really, really want to see you.'

The sweat on his skin was turning to steam, an ever
so light, watery vapour, since it was still, at nine in the
evening, hot enough to make one faint.

'You know something?' Adriana asked, her tone
changing.

'What?'

'Do you remember that uncle and aunt of mine who
were supposed to go back to Milan this afternoon?'

'Yes.' You couldn't have said he wasted words with
Adriana.

'Well, they left the house, but when they got to the airport, they discovered their flight had been cancelled, with all the others, because of a wildcat strike.'

'What did they do?'

'They decided to take the train, poor things. You can imagine what kind of journey they'll have in this heat! Tell me what you were doing.'

'Who — me?' he replied, wrong-footed by the sudden change in subject.

'Would Chief Inspector Salvo Montalbano like to say what he was doing at the moment he received a telephone call from the student Miss Adriana Morreale?'

'I was on my way to the fridge to get something to eat.'

'Where do you eat? In the kitchen, as people who eat alone usually do?'

'I don't like eating in the kitchen.'

'So where do you like to eat?'

'On the veranda.'

'You have a veranda? Fantastic! Do me a favour and lay the table for two.'

'Why?'

'Because I want to be there too.'

'But you just said you couldn't come!'

'No, silly, I meant in my mind. I want you to take a bite from my plate, and I'll take one from yours.'

Montalbano's head was spinning.

'O . . . okay.'

'Bye. And goodnight. I'll phone tomorrow. I love you.'

'Me t—'

'What did you say?'

'Meat. I said "meat". I was just thinking of what I was going to eat.'

He'd saved himself by kicking the ball out.

'Oh, listen, I've just had an idea. Why don't you call me into the station for questioning tomorrow morning and grill me with one of those eye-to-eye investigations like Tommaseo wants to do?' And she hung up laughing.

So much for the refrigerator! So much for eating! The only thing to do, and immediately, was to dive into the sea and go for a long swim, to cool his head and lower the temperature of his blood, which had reached boiling point. Now Adriana, too, was doing her best to turn up the August heat.

*

As he was swimming in the dark of night, a new torment began. It was a sensation he knew well. He turned over to float on his back, eyes open and gazing at the stars.

The sensation was one of a hand drill boring into his brain. And it made the classic sound of a drill with each turn: zzzrr ... zzzrr ... zzzrr ...

This tremendous nuisance – which no longer caused him any surprise, since it had been happening to him for years – meant that at some time during the preceding day he had heard something of great importance, something that might lead to a resolution of the case and to which he had not immediately paid any attention.

But when had he heard it? And who had said it?

Zzzzrr ... zzzrr ... zzzrr ...

Like a woodworm gnawing, making him nervous.

With broad, slow strokes, he returned to shore.

Entering his house, he realized his appetite was gone so he grabbed a new bottle of whisky, a glass and a packet of cigarettes, then went to sit on the veranda, dripping wet, without bothering to take off his swimming trunks.

He racked his brains, but nothing came to him.

After an hour, he gave up. It used to be, he thought, that with a little concentration he could recall what was bothering him. But when, exactly? he asked himself. When you were younger, Montalbà, came the inevitable answer.

He decided to have something to eat. And he remembered that Adriana had asked him to lay a place for her as well ... He was tempted to do so, but felt ridiculous.

He laid the table for himself, went into the kitchen, put his hand on the refrigerator door, still thinking of Adriana, and experienced an electric shock.

How could that be? Apparently the refrigerator wasn't working properly. It was dangerous, in fact. He'd better buy a new one.

But then again, why, though his hand was still on the door, wasn't he still being shocked? Maybe it hadn't been an electrical shock at all, but something inside him, a short-circuit in his head.

He'd felt the shock when he was thinking of Adriana! It was something the girl had said!

He went back out on to the veranda. His appetite had disappeared again.

All at once Adriana's words resurfaced in his mind. He sprang to his feet, grabbed the cigarettes and went to walk along the water's edge.

*

Three hours later, he had finished the packet and his legs ached. He went home, looked at the clock. It was three in the morning. He washed, shaved, got dressed, then drank a mug of coffee. At a quarter to four he went out, got into his car, and drove off.

At that hour he could cruise in the cool of the night. At his customary pace, without needing to race around like Gallo.

He was chasing a hope. One so subtle, so ethereal, that the slightest doubt would make it disappear into thin air. Actually, to tell the truth, he was chasing a wild idea.

*

When he pulled into Punta Raisi airport it was almost eight o'clock in the morning. It had taken him as long as it would a normal driver to make a round trip. But it had been a peaceful ride. He hadn't felt hot and had had no occasion to grumble at any other drivers.

He parked and got out of the car. The air there was

less oppressive than it was in Vigàta. He could actually breathe. The first thing he did was go to the bar: a double espresso, extra strong. Then he went to the airport police station. 'I'm Inspector Montalbano. Is Inspector Capuano there?' Every time he was at the airport for Livia's arrival or departure, he dropped in on Capuano.

'He's just arrived. You can go in, if you like.'

He knocked and entered.

'Montalbano! You waiting for your girlfriend?'

'No, I'm here to ask you to lend me a hand.'

'At your service. What is it?'

Montalbano told him.

'That'll take a little while. But I've got just the right person.' And he called, 'Cammarota!'

He was a thirty-year-old, black as ink, eyes sparkling with intelligence.

'I want you to make yourself available to Inspector Montalbano, who's a friend of mine. You two can stay in here and use my computer. I have to go now and report to the commissioner.'

They remained holed up in Capuano's office till noon, drinking two coffees and two beers each. Cammarota proved competent and clever, telephoning a variety of ministries, airports and airlines. By the end, the inspector knew exactly what he had wanted to know.

When he got back into his car, he sneezed: the delayed effect of the air-conditioning in Capuano's office.

Halfway home, he saw a trattoria with three articulated

lorries parked in front, a sure sign that the food was good. After ordering, he went to make a phone call. 'Adriana? Montalbano here.'

'Oh, goody! Have you decided to give me the third degree?'

'I need to see you.'

'When?'

'This evening, around nine, at my house in Marinella. We'll have dinner there.'

'I hope I can get myself organized in time. Is there any news?'

How had she known? 'I think so.'

'I love you.'

'Don't tell anyone you're coming to my place.'

'You must be joking!'

Then he called Headquarters and asked for Fazio.

'Chief, where are you? I was looking for you this morning because—'

'You can tell me later. I'm on my way back from Palermo and need to talk to you. We'll meet at the station at five. Make sure you drop all other engagements.'

The restaurant had a vast ceiling fan that filled him with joy, allowing him to remain seated without his shirt and underpants sticking to him. As he'd expected, the food was good.

Getting back into the car, he thought that if, when he'd left, his hope had been thin as a cobweb, now, on his return, it was as thick as a rope.

A gallows' rope.

He started singing, as off-key as a dog, 'O Lola', from *Cavalleria Rusticana*.

*

At home in Marinella, he had a shower, put on clean clothes, and headed in haste for the station. He felt feverish and restless, irritated by the slightest thing.

'Aah, Chief, you gotta call from—'

'I don't give a shit. Send me Fazio straight away.'

He turned on the mini-fan. Fazio came running. Curiosity was eating him alive.

'Come in, close the door and sit down.'

Fazio obeyed and sat on the edge of his chair, eyes trained on the inspector. He looked exactly like a hunting dog.

'Did you know there was a strike at Punta Raisi yesterday and most of the flights were cancelled?'

'No, I didn't.'

'I heard it on the regional news report.' It was a lie. He didn't want to tell him he'd heard it from Adriana.

'Okay, Chief, so there was a strike. Who doesn't go on strike, these days? What's that got to do with us?'

'Oh, it's got a lot to do with us. A lot.'

'I get it, Chief. You're beating about the bush to make me stew.'

'So? How many times have you done the same to me?'

'Fine, but now you've had your revenge. Talk.'

'All right. So I heard about the strike but didn't pay any attention. Nevertheless, after a little while, an idea started to form in my head. I thought it over, and all at once everything became clear to me. Crystal clear. So, very early this morning I left for Punta Raisi. I had to see if my initial theory would stand up.'

'And did it?'

'Completely.'

'So?'

'It means I know the name of Rina's killer.'

'Spitaleri,' Fazio said calmly.

EIGHTEEN

'Oh, no, you don't!' Montalbano roared. 'You can't screw up my performance like that! It's not fair! I'm supposed to be the one to say the name! Show more respect for your superiors!'

'I won't say another word,' Fazio promised.

Montalbano calmed down, but Fazio couldn't tell if he was seriously angry or only joking.

'How did you work it out?'

'Chief, you went to Punta Raisi to confirm something. Until proven to the contrary, Punta Raisi is an airport. Now who, among the suspects, got on a plane? Spitaleri. Angelo Speciale and his stepson Ralf went by train. Correct?'

'Correct. So, when I heard the word "strike", it occurred to me that we had always taken for granted that Spitaleri's alibi was true. I had also learned that when our colleagues in Fiacca, who were handling the case of the disappearance, had pressed Spitaleri with questions, he had wriggled out with the story of his trip to Bangkok. And I thought they'd checked it. Which was why we never asked him to prove that he actually left for Bangkok on that day.'

'But, Chief, we have indirect confirmation. Dipasquale and his secretary had a phone call from Spitaleri when he was at a stopover on the way. And I'm convinced that call was made.'

'Yes, but who says it came from a stopover? If you call me long-distance direct from a public phone or mobile, I don't know where you're calling from. You can say you're in Ambaradam or at the Arctic Circle, and I have no choice but to believe you.'

'True.'

'That's why I went to Police Headquarters at Punta Raisi. They were very nice. It took four hours, but I was right on target. That twelfth of October was a Wednesday. The Thai Airways flight takes off from Fiumicino in Rome at two fifteen. Spitaleri leaves for Punta Raisi to catch a plane to Fiumicino that should get him there in time to catch the other flight. But, once at Punta Raisi, he finds out that the plane that's supposed to take him to Rome is delayed for two hours due to technical problems. Therefore he's not going to make it in time to catch the plane to Bangkok. So, he's stranded at Punta Raisi. He manages to get his ticket changed to the next day. Not a big problem. The Thai flight for Thursday leaves Rome at two forty-five in the afternoon. Thus far, we're on safe ground.'

'In what sense?'

ANDREA CAMILLERI

'In the sense that we can document everything I've said. Now I'm going to conjecture. That Spitaleri, having nothing to do in Palermo, returns to Vigàta. I believe he took the Trapani road, which, before getting here, passes Montereale. He decides to see if the work at Pizzo has been finished. Bear in mind that the decision to wait till the following day to bury the illegal apartment was made by Dipasquale, and therefore Spitaleri doesn't know this. When he gets there, everyone's gone: the masons, Speciale, Ralf. He can see, however, that the illegal floor has not been covered. He can still get inside. At this point – and this is my boldest conjecture – he notices Rina in the vicinity. And it must have occurred to him that he himself, at that moment, in that place, did not exist.'

'What do you mean, he didn't exist?'

'Think. There's no way Spitaleri can be at Pizzo at that time of the day. Everyone thinks he's on his way to Bangkok and, what's more, he hasn't yet returned to Vigàta. Therefore no one knows he never left. What better opportunity? He calls his office from his mobile phone. Thus he confirms his alibi. He thinks everything's covered, but he makes a big mistake.'

'Namely?'

'The phone call itself. Apparently it had been at least three months since Spitaleri last went to Bangkok because as of July the Thai Airways flights from Rome became direct. There were no stopovers.'

'And what happened next, in your opinion?'

'Always remember I'm sailing on the seas of hypothesis. Thinking he's safe, he approaches Rina and, when he sees the girl's not interested, he pulls out the knife he always carries with him — which he also pointed at Ralf, as Adriana told us — and forces her into the underground apartment. You can imagine the rest.'

'No,' said Fazio. 'I don't want to imagine it.'

'And this also explains the contract.'

'The one with Speciale?'

'Exactly. The agreement he made with Speciale to sort out the house after the amnesty was granted. One thing about it seemed fishy to me, the bit about Speciale not being allowed to ask any other company to do the work. Spitaleri wanted to be absolutely certain that he would be the one to dig out the illegal floor, which would enable him to get rid of the trunk with the dead girl inside it. This idea occurs to him while he's abroad, and that's why, the moment he gets back, he races over to Speciale's house, hoping he's still in Vigàta. Does that make sense to you?'

'It does.'

'So, in your opinion, what should I do now?'

'What should you do? Tomorrow morning you go to Prosecutor Tommaseo, you tell him the whole story and—'

'I take it you-know-where.'

'Why?'

'Because, since it involves somebody with connections like Spitaleri's, Tommaseo will proceed as if he's walking on eggshells. Not only that. He'll find himself confronted by lawyers who'll eat him raw. Laying hands on Spitaleri means making life unpleasant for too many people – Mafiosi, MPs, mayors. He's got attack dogs all around him.'

'Chief, Tommaseo may have a habit of losing his head with women, but when it comes to integrity—'

'But he'll be surrounded! If you like, I'll give you a little preview of Spitaleri's line of defence.

'"But on the morning of the twelfth, my client left Palermo on an earlier flight than the one that had the breakdown."

'"But Spitaleri's name does not appear in any of the manifests of the earlier flights!"

'"Yes, but Rossi's does!"

'"And who is this Rossi?"

'"A passenger who gave up his seat, allowing Spitaleri to leave earlier to catch the flight to Bangkok."'

'Can I do Tommaseo's part?' asked Fazio.

'Of course.'

'"So how do you explain the telephone call from a stopover that never occurred?"' After asking the question, he eyed the inspector triumphantly.

Montalbano laughed. 'You know how the lawyer will respond? Like this.

'"But my client called from Rome! The Thai flight that day took off at six thirty p.m., not at two fifteen!"'

'Is that really when it left?' asked Fazio.

'Yes. Except that Spitaleri didn't know there would be

a delay. He thought the flight was already on its way to Bangkok.'

Fazio twisted his face doubtfully. 'Of course, when you put it that way . . .'

'Don't you see I'm right? We risk playing follow-up to the Arab mason's number.'

'So, what should we do?'

'We absolutely have to get a confession.'

'Easy to say!'

'Look, there's no guarantee that we'll succeed in sending him to prison even with a confession. He'll say we tortured and beat him into it. A confession is the minimum we need just to take him to court.'

'Okay, but how?'

'I've got a vague idea.'

'Really?'

'Yes. But I don't want to talk about it here. Could we meet at my place tonight, around ten thirty?'

*

It was eight o'clock when he got back to Marinella. The first thing he did was go out on to the veranda.

There wasn't a breath of wind. The air felt like a heavy mantle cast over the earth. The heat absorbed by the sand during the day was only now turning to vapour, making the atmosphere hotter and more humid. The sea seemed dead, the white foam of the surf like drool.

His agitation over Adriana's visit and the things he

would have to ask her made him sweat as much as if he were in a sauna.

He took off his clothes and went to the refrigerator in his underpants. He was dumbstruck. He remembered that he hadn't looked inside it since Adelina had told him she was going to make him enough food for two days. What he was looking at wasn't the inside of a refrigerator, but a corner of La Vuccirìa, the great Palermo market. He inhaled the scent of dish after dish, and it was all still fresh.

He laid the table on the veranda. He brought out green olives, cured black *passuluna* olives, celery, *caciocavallo* cheese, and six dishes, one with fresh anchovies, one with *calamaretti*, another with *purpiteddri*, another with squid, another with tuna and another with sea snails. Each was dressed differently, and there was still more in the fridge.

Afterwards he took a shower and decided to call Livia. He needed to hear her voice at the very least. Perhaps to steel himself for Adriana's imminent visit. He was greeted by the same recording of a woman's voice telling him that the telephone of the person he'd called was either switched off or unobtainable.

Unobtainable! What the hell was that supposed to mean?

And why was Livia making herself unavailable when he needed her most? Couldn't she hear the silent SOS he was sending her? Was the young lady perhaps too distracted by the diversions, indeed the entertainments, provided by Cousin Massimiliano?

As he grew more and more furious, not knowing whether the cause was jealousy or wounded pride, the doorbell rang. He was unable to move. A second ring, longer this time.

Finally he went to open the door, walking like a combination of a condemned man on his way to the electric chair and a fifteen-year-old on his first date, already drenched with sweat.

Adriana, wearing jeans and a blouse, kissed him lightly on the lips, as if they'd long been intimate, and entered the house, brushing against him. How could it be that in this terrible heat the girl always smelled so cool and fresh?

'It took some doing,' she said, 'but I finally made it! Would you believe I feel sort of moved? Let me see it.'

'See what?'

'Your house.'

She had a careful look round, room after room, as if she was going to buy it. 'Which side do you sleep on?' she asked, standing at the foot of the bed.

'Over there. Why?'

'No reason. Just curious. What's your girlfriend's name?'

'Livia.'

'Where's she from?'

'Genoa.'

'Let me see the picture.'

'Of what?'

'Your girlfriend, of course.'

'I haven't got one.'

'Come on, I won't eat it.'

'It's true. I haven't got one.'

'Why not?'

'I don't know.'

'Where is she now?'

'She's away.'

It had slipped out. Adriana gave him a confused look.

'She's on a boat with friends,' he explained. Why hadn't he told her the truth? 'Everything's ready on the veranda. Come,' he said, to steer her away from that delicate subject.

*

On seeing the table, Adriana baulked. 'It's true I like to eat, but all this stuff ... God, it's so beautiful here!'

'You have to sit down first.'

Adriana sat on the bench but slid over only a little, so that for Montalbano to sit, he had practically to press against her.

'I don't like this,' said Adriana.

'You don't like what?'

'Sitting like this.'

'You're right. It's too tight. If you'd just slide over a little ...'

'That's not what I meant. I don't like eating without looking at you.'

Montalbano went to get a chair and sat in front of

her. He, too, felt better with a little distance between them. But how was it that, even as the night progressed, the heat remained so intense?

'May I have a little wine?'

He took out a strong, chilled white. It went down the throat like a dream. There were two more bottles in the refrigerator. 'Before I begin, I must ask you something I'm anxious to know.'

'I haven't got a boyfriend. And I'm not with anyone.'

The inspector felt embarrassed. 'That's not what ... I didn't mean ... Do you know Spitaleri personally?'

'The builder? The one who saved Rina from Ralf? No, we were never introduced.'

'How come? After all, you and your sister lived just a few yards away from his work site.'

'True. But, you see, during that period I was living more with my aunt and uncle in Montelusa than with my parents in Pizzo. I never met him.'

'Are you sure?'

'Yes.'

'What about afterwards? During the search for Rina?'

'My aunt and uncle took me back to Montelusa almost immediately. My parents were too involved with the search – they couldn't sleep, couldn't eat. My aunt and uncle wanted to get me away from that stressful atmosphere.'

'More recently?'

'I don't think so. I didn't go to the funeral. I kept out of the television interviews. Only one newspaper wrote that Rina had a sister, but they didn't specify that we were twins.'

'Shall we start eating?'

'Gladly. Why did you ask me about Spitaleri?'

'I'll tell you later.'

'You said earlier there was some news.'

'We'll talk about that later, too.'

*

They were eating in silence, occasionally looking each other in the eye, when all of a sudden Montalbano felt one of Adriana's knees pressing against his. He spread his legs slightly, and one of hers slid between them. Then, with her other leg, Adriana took one of his prisoner, squeezing it hard.

It was a miracle the wine went down the right way. But the inspector felt a blush rising and got angry with himself.

Later, Adriana gestured towards the sea snails. 'How is one supposed to eat those?'

'You have to pull them out with a big sort of hairpin that I put among the silverware at your place.'

Adriana tried opening one but didn't succeed. 'You do it for me,' she said. Montalbano used the pin, and she opened her mouth to let him feed her. 'Mmm. It's good. More.' Each time she opened her mouth for a snail, Montalbano nearly had a heart attack.

The bottle of wine was empty in a flash.

'I'll open another.'

'No,' said Adriana, squeezing his imprisoned leg, but she must have noticed his anxiety. 'Okay,' she said, liberating him.

Returning with the opened bottle, the inspector didn't sit in the chair but on the bench, beside her.

When they had finished eating, he cleared the table, leaving the bottle and glasses. When he sat down again, Adriana tucked herself under his arm and leaned her head on his shoulder. 'Why do you keep running away?'

Had the moment come to talk seriously? Perhaps that was best, to confront the question head-on. 'Adriana, believe me, I have no desire whatsoever to run away from you. I like you in a way that has rarely happened to me. But do you realize there's a thirty-three-year age difference between us?'

'I'm hardly asking you to marry me.'

'Okay, but it's the same thing. I'm practically antique, and it really doesn't seem right to me that ... Someone the right age, on the other hand...'

'But what's the right age, anyway? Twenty-five? Thirty? Have you seen men of that age? Have you heard them talk? Do you know how they behave? They have no idea about women!'

'To you I'm just a passing fad, but for me, you risk becoming something else entirely. At my age—'

'Enough of the age stuff. And don't imagine I want you the way I might want an ice-cream cone. Speaking of which, have you got any?'

'Ice cream? Yes.'

He took it out of the freezer, but it was so hard he was unable to cut into it. He brought it out on to the veranda. 'Custard and chocolate. Sound okay to you?' he asked, sitting down as before.

And, also as before, she tucked herself under his arm and leaned her head on his shoulder.

In five minutes the ice cream was edible. Adriana ate hers in silence, without changing position.

Then, as Montalbano was pushing away her empty plate, he noticed that the girl was crying. The sound wrung his heart. He tried to make her raise her head from his shoulder so he could look her in the eye, but she resisted. 'There's another thing you have to consider, Adriana. That for years I've been with a woman I love. And I've always tried as best I can to remain faithful to Livia, who is . . .'

'Away,' said Adriana, raising her head and looking him in the eye.

The same thing must have happened to castles under siege during the wars of yesteryear. Their occupants would hold out for a long time against hunger and thirst, pour boiling oil to repel those climbing the walls, and they would seem impregnable. Then a single shot of a catapult, precise and well aimed, would knock down the iron door, and the besiegers would burst in, encountering no more resistance.

Away. That was the key word Adriana had used. What

had the girl heard in that word when he'd used it? His anger? His jealousy? His weakness? His loneliness?

Montalbano embraced her and kissed her. Her lips tasted of custard and chocolate.

It was like plunging into the great August heat.

Then Adriana said, 'Let's go inside.'

They stood up, still embracing, and at that moment the doorbell rang.

'Who can it be?' asked Adriana.

'It's ... it's Fazio. I told him to come. I'd forgotten about it.'

Without a word, Adriana went to lock herself in the bathroom.

*

As soon as he set foot on the veranda Fazio, seeing the two glasses and the two small ice-cream dishes, asked, 'Is someone else here?'

'Adriana.'

'Ah. And is she leaving now?'

'No.'

'Ah.'

'Like a glass of wine?'

'No, sir, thanks.'

'Some ice cream?'

'No, sir, thanks.'

Clearly he was irritated by the girl's presence.

NINETEEN

They'd been sitting on the veranda for nearly an hour, but even as the night advanced, it brought no relief. In fact, it seemed hotter than ever, as if that wasn't a half-moon in the sky but the midday sun.

When he'd finished talking, he looked inquisitively at Fazio. 'What do you think?' he said.

'You'd like to call Spitaleri into the station for questioning, subject him to one of those interrogations that last a day and a night, and then, when he's reduced to the state of a doormat, have Miss Adriana, whom he's never seen before, suddenly appear before him. Is that what you're saying?'

'More or less.'

'And you think that when he sees the twin sister of the girl he killed standing in front of him he'll crack and confess?'

'I'm hoping that's what he'll do.'

Fazio pursed his lips.

'Not convinced?'

'Chief, the man's a crook. He's got skin thicker than an armadillo's. The moment you call him in for questioning, he'll go on the defensive and put on his armour because he'll expect the works from you. Even if he sees the girl and has a heart attack, I'm sure he won't let it show.'

'So you think it'd be pointless for Adriana to appear?'

'No, I think it might be useful, but that it would be a mistake for it to happen at the police station.'

Adriana, who'd been silent up until then, finally spoke. 'I agree with Fazio. It's the wrong setting.'

'What would be the right one, in your opinion?'

'The other day I suddenly realized that after the amnesty is granted other people will move into that house and live there. And it didn't seem right to me. The idea that others might ... I don't know ... laugh and sing ... in the same living room where Rina had her throat slashed ...'

She made a sort of sobbing sound. Instinctively Montalbano put his hand on hers. Fazio noticed, but showed no surprise.

Adriana pulled herself together. 'I've decided to talk to Papa about it.'

'What do you want to do?'

'I'll suggest that he should sell our house and buy the one in which Rina died. Then the illegal apartment will never be lived in by anyone, and my sister's memory will remain free.'

'And what do you expect to achieve by this?'

'You mentioned the exclusive contract Spitaleri has for refurbishing the house. Well, tomorrow morning I'm going to that agency to tell that man— What's his name?'

'Callara.'

'I'm going to tell Callara we want to buy the house, even before the amnesty is granted. We'll deal with the paperwork and cover the amnesty. I'll explain to him why, and let him know that we're willing to pay well for it. I'll convince him, I'm sure. Then I'll ask him to give me keys to the upstairs apartment and to recommend somebody to handle the renovation downstairs. At which point Callara will give me Spitaleri's name. I'll get the phone number and then—'

'Wait a minute. What if Callara wants to come with you?'

'He won't if I don't tell him exactly when I'm going. He can't remain at my disposal for two whole days. Anyway, I think the fact that we own a house just a few yards away from his will work in my favour.'

'And then what?'

'I'll phone Spitaleri and ask him to come out to Pizzo. If I can manage to be downstairs, in the living room where he murdered Rina, at the moment he arrives, and he sees me there for the first time—'

'You can't be left alone with Spitaleri!'

'I won't be alone if you're hiding behind that stack of window frames.'

'How do you know there are frames in the living room?' asked an alert Fazio, like the smart cop he always was, even in friendly surroundings.

'I told her,' Montalbano cut in.

Silence fell over the three.

'If we take all the necessary precautions,' the inspector said a moment later, 'we could maybe pull it off.'

'Chief, may I speak freely?' Fazio asked.

'Of course.'

'With all due respect to the young lady, I don't like the idea.'

'Why not?' asked Adriana.

'It's extremely dangerous, miss. Spitaleri always goes about with a knife in his pocket, and the man is capable of anything.'

'But if Salvo is there too, it seems to me—'

Fazio didn't show any surprise at that 'Salvo' either.

'I still don't like it. It's not right for us to put you in danger.'

They discussed things for another half-hour. In the end, it was Montalbano who decided. 'We'll do as Adriana suggested. For additional security, you'll be in the vicinity, too, Fazio, perhaps with another of our men.'

'Whatever you say, sir,' said Fazio, surrendering.

He stood up, said goodbye to Adriana and headed for

the door, with the inspector following. But before he left, he looked Montalbano in the eye. 'Chief, think long and hard about it before you give the final go-ahead.'

'Come and sit down,' Adriana said, when Montalbano returned.

'I'm a little tired,' he said.

Something had changed, and the girl knew it.

＊

In his lonely bed, between sweat-dampened sheets, Montalbano had a wretched night, feeling one minute like an utter fool, the next like San Luigi Gonzaga or Sant'Alfonso Maria de' Liguori, someone like that.

＊

Adriana's first call to Montalbano came into the station at around five o'clock the next afternoon. 'I got the keys from Callara. He's thrilled about selling. He must be rather greedy because when he heard that we'd absorb all the costs of the amnesty he practically got down on his knees to thank me.'

'Did he tell you about Spitaleri?'

'He even showed me the contract he'd made with Speciale, and gave me Spitaleri's mobile-phone number into the bargain.'

'Have you rung him?'

'Yes. We made an appointment to meet at the house

tomorrow evening at seven. So, where do we stand with our plan?'

'We'll meet at the house tomorrow around five p.m. That should give us enough time to get everything set up.'

*

Her second call, on the other hand, was to Marinella, around ten o'clock that evening.

'The nurse has just arrived. She's going to stay the night. Can I come and see you?'

What did that mean? Did she want to spend the night with him? Was she joking? He couldn't handle another night playing the part of St Anthony being tempted by demons in the desert. 'Look, Adriana, I—'

'I feel extremely nervous and need some company.'

'I understand perfectly. I'm nervous too.'

'I'll just come for a midnight swim. Come on.'

'Why don't you go to bed? Tomorrow will be a hard day.'

She giggled. 'No problem, I'll bring my swimsuit.'

'Oh, all right.' Why had he given in? Weariness? Because of the heat, which killed the will? Or simply because, really and truly, he felt like seeing her?

*

The girl swam like a dolphin. And Montalbano experienced a new, troubling pleasure, feeling that young body beside his, making the same movements as if it was long accustomed to swimming with him.

Adriana, moreover, had so much stamina she could have swum all the way to Malta. At a certain point, Montalbano couldn't go any further and flipped over to do the dead man's float. She came back and floated beside him.

'Where did you learn to swim?'

'I had a lot of lessons when I was little. When I come here in the summer I spend all day in the water. In Palermo I go to the pool twice a week.'

'Do you do a lot of sport?'

'I go to the gym. I can even shoot.'

'Really?'

'Yes. I used to have a ... well, let's call him a boyfriend. He was a fanatic. He used to take me to the Poligono.'

A pang, ever so slight. Not of jealousy, but of envy for the boy, her former, well, let's call him her lover, who was the right age and could enjoy her company without complications.

'Shall we go back?' said Adriana.

They took their time swimming to the shore. Neither wanted to break the sort of spell that had fallen over their bodies, which they couldn't see in the darkness but could therefore feel all the more through their breathing and the occasional moments of contact.

Then, about two or three yards from the beach, where

the water was waist-deep, Adriana, who was holding Montalbano's hand as she walked, slammed her foot against a metal jerry-can that some idiot had thrown into the water, and fell forward. Instinctively, Montalbano gripped her fingers, but then, perhaps because he lost his balance, he fell in turn, right on top of her.

They resurfaced in each other's clutches as though wrestling, and breathless as if after a long submersion. Adriana slipped again, and they both collapsed under water, still in each other's arms. They emerged even more tightly embraced, then drowned themselves once and for all in other waters.

*

When, much later, Adriana finally left, another nasty night began for Montalbano. He spent it thrashing back and forth, tossing and turning, burning up.

The heat, naturally. And guilt, of course. Perhaps even shame. A hint of self-loathing as well. And throw in a pinch of remorse.

Above all, however, a deep melancholy over a question that had treacherously caught him off-guard: *If you hadn't been fifty-five years old, would you have been able to say no? Not to Adriana, but to yourself? To which the answer could only be: Yes, I would have been able to say no. After all, I've done so before.*

So why did you give in to a part of yourself that you've always been able to control?

Because I'm not as strong as I was. And I knew it.

*So it was the very awareness of approaching old age that made you
weak in front of Adriana's youth and beauty?*

And this time, too, the bitter answer was yes.

*

'Chief, wha'ss wrong?'

'Why?'

'Y'oughta see your face! You feel ill?'

'I didn't sleep, Cat. Get me Fazio.'

Fazio didn't look too pretty either. 'Chief, I didn't
sleep a wink all night. Are you sure about what we're
doing?'

'I'm not sure about anything. But it's the only way.'

Fazio threw up his hands.

'Post a guard at the house. I wouldn't want some idiot
entering the illegal apartment and screwing everything up.
Tell him to leave at five, since by that time we'll be there.
Also, get your hands on a twenty-yard extension cable
with a three-outlet adaptor, and buy three mechanic's
lamps from the repair shop. You know the kind that have
a protective grating for the bulb?'

'Yessir. But what's all this for?'

'We'll hook into the power from the socket next to
the front door and bring it down into the illegal apartment, as Callara did when he took that builder there.
We'll plug the three mechanic's lamps into the adaptor,
two of which will go in the living room. At least there'll
be some light.'

'But won't all this make Spitaleri suspicious?'

'Adriana can always tell him Callara suggested it. Who you going to bring with you?'

'Galluzzo.'

＊

He was unable to do anything. He took no calls, signed no papers. He kept his head close to the mini-fan. At moments, images of himself and Adriana from the night before came into his mind, and he immediately blotted them out. He wanted to concentrate on what might happen with Spitaleri, but he couldn't. Above all else, the sun that day would have roasted a lizard. It was like when, towards the end of a fireworks display, the most colourful rockets burst in the sky with the most powerful explosions; in the same way August, during its later phase, was firing its most torrid, scorching days at them.

After he didn't know how long, Fazio came in and told him he had everything. 'It's deadly outside, Chief.'

They reconfirmed their plan to meet at the house at five.

The inspector didn't feel like leaving the office to eat. He wasn't even hungry. 'Catarella, don't put any calls through and don't let anyone into my office.'

Once more, he locked his door, took off his clothes, pointed the mini-fan at the armchair, which he had pulled up to the desk, and sat down. A little later he nodded off.

When he woke it was four o'clock. He went into the

271

bathroom, stripped naked, washed himself with water so warm it felt like piss, put his clothes back on, went out, got into his car and headed for Pizzo.

*

Adriana and Fazio's cars were parked in front of the house. Before he got out, he opened the glove compartment, took out his pistol and slipped it into the back pocket of his trousers.

They were all in the living room. Adriana smiled and shook hands with him. This time her hand was ice cold, a relief. Was the formality for Galluzzo's benefit?

'Fazio, did you bring the equipment?'

'Yessir.'

'Hook up the lights at once.'

Fazio and Galluzzo left. They were barely out of the door when Adriana came over and hugged him. 'I love you even more today.' And she kissed him.

He managed to resist, gently pushing her away. 'Adriana, try to understand. I have to be lucid.'

Slightly disappointed, the girl went out on to the terrace. He rushed into the kitchen. Luckily there was a bottle of cold water in the refrigerator. To avoid complications, he didn't move from that spot. A few minutes later, he heard Galluzzo calling, 'Chief, come and have a look.'

He went out on to the terrace. 'Come with me,' he said to Adriana.

Fazio had placed a lamp just outside the small bath-room and the other two in the living room. The light barely sufficed to let one see where one was stepping, and people's faces were like frightening masks: the eyes disap-peared, the mouths were like black holes, the shadows on the walls loomed large and menacing. Just as on the set of a horror film. It was stifling down there – one could barely breathe. It was like being in a submarine that had long been under water.

'Okay,' said Montalbano. 'Let's go.'

Once outside, he said, 'Let's move the cars. Only the young lady's car should be in front of the house. Adriana, give me the keys to your house.'

He took them and gave them to Fazio. Then he pulled out the keys to his car and handed them to Galluzzo. 'You take mine. Park them behind Adriana's house so that they can't be seen from the road. Then go inside and watch for Spitaleri's car from two different windows. As soon as you see it, Fazio will warn me with one ring on my mobile phone and come running. Is that clear? By the time Spitaleri goes downstairs, both of you should already be here and positioned in such a way that, no matter what happens, he can't escape. Is that clear?'

'Perfectly,' said Fazio.

*

They sat on the sofa in each other's arms and didn't say a word. Not because they had nothing to say to one another,

273

but because they felt it was better so. At a certain point the inspector glanced at his watch. 'Just ten more minutes. Maybe we'd better go downstairs.'

Adriana grabbed her bag, with the house documents inside, and slung it across her chest.

When they were in the illegal living room, Montalbano tried to hide behind the window frames. There wasn't much room – they were too close to the wall. Sweating and cursing, he pushed them forward, making them lean a bit. He tried again and felt more comfortable; he could move without hindrance. 'Can you see me?' he asked Adriana.

No answer. He stuck his head out and saw the girl swaying in the middle of the room, like a tree in the wind. He realized that, at the last minute, Adriana had been seized by a fit of panic. He ran to her and she embraced him, trembling. 'I'm afraid, so afraid.'

She seemed very upset. Montalbano was calling himself a fool. He hadn't thought of the effect that being in that place would have on the girl's nerves. 'Let's drop every-thing and leave.'

'No,' she said. 'Wait.'

She was making an enormous effort to control herself, and it showed.

'Give me ... give me your gun.'

'Why?'

'Let me hold it. It'll make me feel safer. I'll put it in my bag.'

Montalbano pulled out the weapon, but didn't hand it over. He was undecided. 'Adriana, you must realize that—'

At that moment they heard Spitaleri's voice nearby: 'Miss Morreale? Are you here?'

He must have been calling from the window of the small bathroom. Why hadn't the inspector's mobile phone worked? Were they out of range down there? With one swift motion Adriana took the gun from his hand and put it into her bag.

'I'm here, Mr Spitaleri,' she said, suddenly calm, her voice sounding almost cheerful.

Montalbano had barely time to hide. He heard Spitaleri's footsteps as he entered the living room. And again Adriana's voice, this time transformed, silvery, like that of the adolescent she'd once been. 'Come, Michele.'

How did she know Spitaleri's first name? Had she read it in the documents Callara had given her? And why such familiarity?

Then there was silence. What was happening? And, suddenly, a laugh, but broken, like pieces of glass falling to the floor. Was it Adriana's? Then, finally, Spitaleri's voice: 'You ... you're not ...?'

'Do you want to try again? Hm? Go ahead, Michele. Look. How do you like me?'

Montalbano heard a sound of ripping fabric. *Matre santa*, what was Adriana doing?

Then Spitaleri bellowed, 'I'll kill you too! Slut! You're an even bigger whore than your sister!'

275

ANDREA CAMILLERI

Montalbano leaped out. Adriana had torn open her blouse and her breasts were hanging out. Spitaleri, knife in hand, was advancing towards her, walking stiffly, like a mechanical puppet.

'Stop!' the inspector shouted.

But Spitaleri didn't hear him. He took another step, and Adriana fired. A single shot. Straight to the heart, as she'd practised at the Poligono. As Spitaleri fell onto the trunk, Montalbano ran to Adriana and grabbed the pistol from her. Face to face, they eyed one another. And, feeling the ground give way under his feet, the inspector understood.

Fazio and Galluzzo came running in, weapons in hand, and froze.

'He tried the same thing with her,' said Montalbano, as Adriana was trying to cover her breasts with her torn blouse, 'so I was forced to shoot him. Look, he's still holding the knife.'

Throwing the gun to the floor, he left the room and, outside the illegal apartment, started running as if he was being chased. He raced down the stone staircase, two steps at a time, to the beach, where, all at once, he tore off his clothes, not giving a damn about the couple staring at him in shock, and dived into the sea.

*

He swam and he wept. Out of anger, humiliation, shame, disappointment, wounded pride.

For not having realized that Adriana was using him to achieve her end, which was to kill with her own hands the man who had slashed her sister's throat.

With the phoney 'I love you', the phoney passion, the phoney fear, she had led him step by step where she wanted to go. He had been a puppet in her hands.

All theatre. All make-believe.

While he, dazzled by beauty and lost in pursuit of intoxicating youth, had fallen for it, at fifty-five years of age and more, like a child.

He swam and he wept.

NOTES

page 3 – ... *her Joyful and not-so-Joyful Mysteries* – the Joyful Mysteries represent five of the traditional fifteen Mysteries of the Rosary, with the other ten consisting of the five Sorrowful Mysteries and the five Glorious Mysteries. In 2002 Pope John Paul II added five new 'optional' Mysteries, the Luminous Mysteries. The Joyful Mysteries concern the early episodes in the life of Christ and the Virgin Mary, namely the Annunciation, the Visitation, the Nativity, the Presentation of Jesus in the Temple, and the Finding of Jesus in the Temple.

page 32 – '*I don't want the media finding out – heaven forbid that this should turn into another Vermicino*' – Montalbano is alluding to the harrowing three-day ordeal of Alfredino Rampi, a six-year-old boy who fell into an artesian well only ten inches wide and ninety yards deep in the township of Vermicino near Rome in June 1981. The event was covered non-stop for eighteen hours by the three national RAI television stations and ended in tragedy. After two failed attempts at rescue in which Alfredino fell further down into the well, he was found dead at the third attempt, probably from injuries sustained in his repeated falls.

page 40 – '*... this government has granted amnesty after amnesty*' – the fire chief is alluding to certain policies of the government of media tycoon Silvio Berlusconi, which granted amnesty on a variety of fiscal and other violations, including those of tax dodgers who parked vast sums of money in financial havens abroad and those of builders who had ravaged much of the landscape, especially in the south of Italy, with illegal constructions in violation of zoning codes.

page 42 – ... *said Gallo in perfect Italian* – the reader should bear in mind that much of the dialogue in this and other of Camilleri's books, and some of the narrative, is in Sicilian dialect or a blend of Sicilian and Italian. In this particular context the use of Italian serves to alert the peasant to the fact that he is dealing with figures of authority, namely the police.

page 85 – '*Don't you pay for protection?*' – that is, Mafia 'protection'. In the original, Camilleri uses the word *pizzo* (which literally means 'point' or 'tip'), the Sicilian term used for the pay-off required of businesses operating on Mafia turf. There is perhaps a little irony in the author's also calling the district in which the illegally built house is situated Pizzo, which in this case refers no doubt to the promontory or 'point' on which it stands.

page 106 – '*... the period of co-operation between all the different commissariats regardless of territorial boundaries*' – in the Italian police bureaucracy the administrative term for a police department the size of that under Montalbano's direct authority is *commissariato*, and the various *commissariati* fall under the authority of the *questura*, here represented by the commissioner's office in Montelusa. Normally the chain of command and jurisdiction is determined territorially, but during the period alluded to by Fazio, the *commissariati* of different jurisdictions were supposed to 'cooperate', leading, Italian-style, to a great deal of confusion.

page 113 – Ah, servile Italy … a brothel! – *Purgatorio* 77, 6; my translation.

page 113 – Italy was still servile … thanks to a helmsman whom she would have been better off without – The 'helmsman' being, of course, Silvio Berlusconi.

page 116 – **Lupus in fabula** – Latin: literally, 'a wolf in the story'; the figurative meaning is the same as 'speak of the devil'.

page 125 – 'But tomorrow is the fifteenth of August!' – 15 August is Ferragosto, the biggest holiday of the summer.

page 136 – 'Better sunstroke than looking like somebody going to the Pontida meetings' – Montalbano is referring to the politicians of the secessionist extreme-right Lega Nord (Northern League), who stage their political summits at Pontida in northern Italy and are fond of wearing baseball caps.

page 136 – **'Vocumprà?'** – a common refrain recited by foreign street pedlars in Italy, usually of North African or sub-Saharan origin. The word is a corruption of the phrases *Vuoi comprare* or *Vuole comprare*, which mean, 'Do you want to buy?'

page 171 – … a quatrain by Pessoa: Fernando Pessoa (1888–1935) was Portugal's greatest modern poet.

page 194 – … he was behaving like the soldier who doesn't want to go to war – a reference to the Sicilian expression *fari u fissu pri nun iri a la guerra*, which means to feign ignorance to avoid doing something unpleasant. Literally, the phrase means 'to pretend to be stupid to avoid going to war'.

page 211 – 'Maybe we ought to use little folded-up pieces of paper, like Provenzano' – Montalbano is referring to the famous *pizzini* of Bernardo Provenzano, the Mafia 'boss of bosses' arrested in 2006 after forty-three years on the run. Provenzano used these little folded-up messages to communicate his orders to the various agents of his crime network. In an 21 April 2006 op-ed in the *New York Times*, written on the occasion of Provenzano's arrest, Camilleri stated:

> The authorities said that Mr Provenzano would transmit his orders — regarding such matters as who should be rewarded with government contracts, whom one should vote for in local and national elections, how one should act on specific occasions — by means of *pizzini*, little scraps of paper folded several times over, which his trusty couriers (mostly peasants with spotless records) would pass from hand to hand along lengthy, circuitous and seemingly random routes. These were necessary precautions to reduce, as much as possible, the risk of interception. One *pizzino*, for example, took more than forty-eight hours to travel the mile between the boss's cottage and Corleone. Others could take weeks to reach a nearby destination. The telephone was out of the question. In every *pizzino*, there was always a mention of God and his will and protection [...]

In 2007 Camilleri published a book on Provenzano's *pizzini* entitled *Voi non sapete* ('You don't know') in which he explains, in the form of a dictionary, some sixty of the Sicilian words most frequently used by the crime boss. The book's title refers to Provenzano's statement to the authorities upon arrest, in which he was alluding to the Mafia war that he thought would break out after his removal from power. All proceeds from the book go to a charitable organization founded to help victims of Mafia violence.

Notes by Stephen Sartarelli